The Half-Breed Gunslinger

The Half-Breed Gunslinger I

Bret Lee Hart

The Half-Breed Gunslinger
The Half-Breed Gunslinger I
Copyright 2012, 2022 Bret Lee Hart
ISBN-13: 9798820451355
Cover Art Copyright 2022 Laura Shinn Designs
http://laurashinn.yolasite.com
(Revised cover & formatting, 2022)

The Half-Breed Gunslinger is a work of fiction. Though actual locations may be mentioned, they are used in a fictitious manner and the events and occurrences were invented in the mind and imagination of the author except for the inclusion of actual historical facts. Similarities of characters or names used within to any person – past, present, or future – are coincidental except where actual historical characters are purposely interwoven.

THE HALF-BREED GUNSLINGER
The Half-Breed Gunslinger I

In 1860 there was more open range cattle in Florida than in Texas and all the other states combined. It took a special breed of man to live there, and an even harder man to survive.

Hunter James Dolin, half white and half Indian, was such a man. He was a gambler by trade and a gunslinger of necessity and attracted trouble wherever he traveled. But with his 2 Colt Walkers and Bowie knife, he could handle almost anything.

A loner, he's matchless when it comes to a fight of any kind-but can he outgun the private armies of two powerful tycoons who unite for a single purpose?

❦*❧

FORWARD

The year was 1860. Some of the white men of these times were outlaws who dwelt in the swamps far south of the Carolinas, trying to make a living any way they could. Most of them were out-of-work soldiers, since the surrender and removal of Chief Billy Bowlegs, leader of the Seminole Indian Tribe, which brought the end of the third and last of the Seminole Indian Wars. This left much land for the taking.

These same men worked as hired gunmen for cattle ranchers, who found themselves in a power struggle over these lands. With the Indian Wars all but over, most of the armies moved north out of Florida, leaving it lawless.

All but a few hundred Seminoles remained in the southern swamp territories. These Indians, along with other tribes, were intermingled with runaway Negro slaves who would not surrender to the Northern Armies. They retreated deep into the swamps to avoid relocation or death. The swamps in these parts were brutal. Gators, snakes, and insects made their home here.

There was more open range cattle in Florida than in Texas and all the other states combined. The men who drove these cows were called 'crackers', from the cracks of their whips they used to move the herds. Some were honest men and some were rustlers and murderers, depending on who they rode for.

With the election of the first Republican President, a congressman named Abraham Lincoln, talk of abolishing slavery seemed to be pushing the country toward instability. War between all the states was brewing, making the future of the south uncertain. The only thing for certain around these parts – men lived and died by the gun, taking what they wanted, or they died trying.

October's dry air temporarily pushed the mosquitoes deep into the marshes that in summertime were said to be thick enough to choke out herds of cattle. It took a special breed of man to live here, and an even harder man to survive.

CHAPTER ONE

Hunter James Dolin, a man in his prime, half-white, half-Indian, was a gambler by choice and a gunslinger of necessity. He headed south; the massive rains had brought the swamps further inland, but the ridge he traveled was high for this area. There were many different kinds of trees on this trail, great oaks, yellow pine, and Australian pines, as well. The path was fairly narrow and curvy, intertwining between them.

Now that the wind and rain were dying down and the first signs of daybreak was appearing through the trees, those three outlaws would surely start hunting him again. He felt they were close.

About ninety miles back and a few days earlier, in the Crackerjack Saloon along the Withlacoochee River, Dolin's ace-high straight flush had beat one of the three outlaws' full house. He won fair and square – two ounces of gold and a just 'broke in' Henry rifle. These days that was more than reason enough to kill a man.

Hunter had felt the itch in his craw that warned him he had out-stayed his welcome, and knew it was high time for him to leave this place. Without taking his eyes off the men at the poker table, Hunter had gathered up his winnings, while he spoke, "Thank you, Gentlemen. It's been a pleasure."

The man at the table to Hunter's left, the one who just lost his Henry rifle, had stood and replied angrily, "Do you think we're just gonna' let you walk on out of here, half-breed?"

"Easy, Billy," said a man the others called Jed. He had sat across the rickety wood card table from Hunter. "We're dealing with a man that's awful lucky, or very good – not sure which."

Hunter had stood, slung his saddlebags over his shoulder, and then picked up his rifle without reply.

"Which way you headin', mister?" asked Jed.

"Not sure yet, just wanderin'."

"Just wanderin', huh? Well, you be careful, there's a lot of bad men hereabouts."

"Thanks for the warnin'," Hunter had said, with a tip of his hat to the third man, who had yet to speak. Hunter slowly backed his way out the front swinging doors of the old rustic saloon, and stepped out into the rain.

"What the devil, Jed?" yelled Billy, slamming his fist on the card strewn table, "We just gonna' let him go?"

"Shut up, stupid! We ain't lettin' nobody go. We're gonna' give him a day's ride to forget about us, then we'll track him down, kill him, get our gold back."

"And my rifle, Jed, don't forget 'bout my rifle."

◆❖◆

The rain had come down hard for three days now, the wind was steady. It had been a hell of a storm, but these men were determined to finish what they had started.

Hunter hid his Appaloosa and his packhorse in a natural cave of vines and pine needles that draped over several, large yellow pine trees. He was determined to draw first blood. Hunter knew from experience that the attacker had the advantage over the attacked. On foot, he took with him the sawed-off double-barreled shotgun. Strapped around his waist he wore two forty-four Colt Walker revolvers, along with a thirteen-inch Bowie knife he kept tucked in the front of his belt.

A hundred paces down the trail, he found a forty-foot oak tree and climbed, stopping a little less than halfway up. There he waited, squatting on a large branch, with killing on his mind and determined to survive at all costs.

He didn't have long to wait. They came up the trail single file, moving slowly on horseback – a perfect scenario for an Indian style ambush. Well, a half-Indian ambush in Hunter's case. The path was located directly under the tree branch where he quietly waited.

The first two men passed by, the man named Jed leading the way. Hunter dropped off the branch onto the third man, Bowie knife in hand. He buried the knife to the hilt between the neck and shoulder bone. By the amount of hot blood that flowed over Hunters' hands and the amount splattering his chest, he figured the knife must have pierced the man's jugular vein.

One down, two to go, ran through the gunslinger's mind.

The momentum of the jump took him and the bleeding body off the other side of the horse, onto the ground. As they were falling, Hunter caught a glimpse of a fourth rider, lagging behind and bringing up the rear, The planned ambush had been for three horseman, but it was too late to change it now. He would follow his plan and worry about the straggler when needed.

Hunter hit the forest floor and rolling to one knee, he pulled the double-barreled shotgun from his side shoulder holster. He blasted the second rider, the man named Billy, with both barrels as he was turning, the shrapnel taking out the man's throat.

That's two down, Hunter counted to himself.

Luckily, the first rider Jed, caught some of the buckshot, which slowed him just enough. Dropping the sawed off shotgun from his right hand, Hunter drew a Colt with his left. He shot Jed three times in the chest, knocking him off the horse to the ground, dead.

Three down, one to go, thought Hunter.

Suddenly, from Hunter's left there came a flash of light instantaneously followed by the sound of gunfire, and then a yell of pain. The yell had come from his own lips. The unexpected fourth and last rider, the one who should have been taken out first, blasted Hunter's revolver out of his left hand, along with the tip of his middle finger.

Hunter quickly drew his right-handed Colt, but before he could turn, the fourth rider spoke, stopping him in his tracks.

"Drop the gun, or I'll kill you right here and now."

Hunter turned his head slowly; he looked up at the tall thin man on the horse, who he had not seen before. It had been a long time since the man's face had known a straight razor, and Hunter couldn't tell if he was Cajun or just hadn't taken a bath for a long spell.

Without making any sudden moves, Hunter said, "You can kill me now 'cause I'm not givin' up my gun."

"You will give'r up," demanded the man on the horse, "One way or the other."

With a deadly stare at the man, Hunter continued in a calm and steady voice, "I don't know you, Mister, but you best think about this – is your life worth two ounces of gold?"

Before his question could be answered, Hunter swung his gun around, launching himself into a turning roll, coming upright quick, firing, shooting the man between the eyes. The Cajun went backwards off his horse and to the ground, a red hole forming on his forehead. He managed to get off a shot as he fell, his bullet missing its target, ricocheting off the tip of Hunter's left boot.

The woods went eerily still and silent, along with the Cajun's heart.

Hunter got to his feet, blood dripping from his hand. He picked up his other revolver off the wet leafy ground, along with his shotgun. He then went over to the dead man sheathing his knife in his neck and retrieved it. He walked down the path to the pine tree cave and entered, pulling a bandana and a bottle of whiskey off the packhorse. Taking a long swig off the bottle, and then soaking the rag with whiskey, he wrapped up his bloody stub of a finger. His breathing returned to normal and Hunter leaned tiredly, back first, against the nearest pine, sliding down to a sitting position just seconds before passing clean out...

CHAPTER TWO

Dark now, many hours had passed. Hunter woke with a jerk from a deep sleep to the sound of a screeching owl. No matter how many times he'd been woken by the owl's shrill scream, it still made him grab the butt of his gun in a moment of distress. After realizing the owl meant him no harm, he knew he must get moving before anyone wandered by, and discovered what went on here. Without wasting more time, he gathered up his belongings.

Able to round up two of the dead men's horses, he rummaged through their saddlebags. He took what little food they contained, a small sack of horse grain, and some jerky. He went through the dead men's pockets. The only one holding money was Jed, the leader of this bunch, who had two gold coins in his trousers.

Four men dead over a card game, Hunter thought as he worked, *what a damn shame,* then a grin appeared on his face. *I guess I would trade an ace-high, straight flush for the lives of them four scoundrels anytime.*

He dragged the bodies into the pine tree cave, along with their gear before setting their horses free. The gear and animals were worth much, but having them in his possession would require an explanation. He didn't take anything that was marked or recognizable. The killings were justified, but it was his word against four deceased white men. Who would believe a half-breed? The reward was not worth the risk. He thought of scalping the men to make it look like an Indian attack, but if the scalps were ever found, it could be evidence against him. Instead, he mounted his horse and headed south, down the trail deeper into the swamps, leaving the bodies to the mercy of the Turkey buzzards, critters, and the worms.

The rain continued to fall at a steady drizzle, fueled by a cold front from the north, beating back the southern winds. There would be no bedding down so he napped in the saddle from time to time as he moved along. This went on until Hunter was two days away from the gun battle and the four rotting corpses. Living on jerked beef and whiskey was fine, but he must hunt soon.

The half-breed pondered in his mind what had happened back on the trail. He knew that the Seminole Indians wouldn't mind him killing four white men, but the Army might. He had heard rumors the blue coats had pretty much packed up and left the state. Then again, these were just rumors and, until he knew for sure, he would have to remain cautious. This would not be a problem for the gunslinger. Caution was second nature to him, and it would be his middle name, if James was not.

Hunter had spent three years tracking Indians out west for the United States Army, but that was a long time ago. He was in his early teens when he left Florida, heading north, then out west. Some said he was searching for his father. If you asked him, he would say a man doesn't need a reason to wander; a man just needs the drive in his soul.

The westward movement had sparked this inside many-a-man in years past. Even so, he knew it was the mixed blood flowing through his veins which gave him such a passion for travel. In a sense he was always running, never from trouble, but toward it. His mother was a Lower Creek Indian who had died during his birth. His father had been rumored to be James

Dolin, a known soldier turned bank robber and gunfighter. He was a half-breed, sometimes accepted by all, but mostly accepted by none. This made Hunter James Dolin one of the toughest men of his time.

As the rain suddenly stopped falling, he found himself riding upon a grassy field. Then he saw movement. Dusk was approaching, a perfect time for hunting rabbit. He dismounted the Appaloosa, thinking it would be best to stay quiet and not attract any unwanted attention.

He unstrapped his bow and notched an arrow. Pulling back the bowstring, he shot one of the many rabbits he saw feeding along the tree line. His arrow flew true, hitting its target just below the ear. A perfect head shot. While retrieving the animal, Hunter stumbled across a small clearing in the woods just off the trail. He started a small fire there with the lighter'd knot he always carried in his saddlebags.

The lighter'd knot, or stump wood, was found at the base of the southern pine tree. After the tree's death, all the sap runs to its bottom. This wood can be dug out just below the ground. With the touch of a lit match, this fueled root will catch fire, making it possible to burn the wet wood of the swamp.

He skinned the varmint with the skill of a slaughterer. He used the same arrow that made the kill as a spit, cooking its flesh to medium. This took a while, but the gunslinger was patient, and the ground was a nice change from the saddle. He then gobbled up the meat feverishly, leaving nothing but bones.

After lighting a cigar from a burning stick from the fire, he redressed his wound. The fingertip was healing nicely, but it still throbbed frequently. The gunslinger could handle the pain, for he had built up quite a tolerance over the years. The itching was the worst as it seemed the part of his finger needing scratching was the missing piece. Hunter found this strange, but at the same time, this was reassuring. In this day and age, he knew more men died from infection, setting in on an open wound, than they did in any other way. Another good excuse to always have whiskey on hand – for sterilization, of course.

Spreading the coals of the fire around and covering them with a layer of dirt, he made a warm dry area to lay out a blanket. This he learned from the Northern Indians, who spent half their year dealing with snow. But it also worked well here, on the wet, cold grounds of the southern swamps. The trick was to make sure to put the right amount of dirt down between yourself and the hot coals, or you just might wake up with your clothes on fire. With one ear open for the slightest sound and his hat covering his face to block the moonlight, he slept through the remainder of the night. No dreams came to him, this was a good sign.

◆❖◆

He awoke with the sun. The cold, dry air from the north had pushed the humidity deeper into the swamps. Hunter felt refreshed after finally getting a good night of sleep. He buried the coals from the fire further and brushed away all signs of his camp before packing up and moving on.

◆❖◆

Two more days and nights of travel had passed. The only thing that crossed his path during this time was a small doe he arrow shot. After skinning the carcass, he carved out some steaks and stripped the rest for jerky. The steaks were packed in salt to delay rot. The jerky was salted and slowly dried in a smoker he made from bamboo.

Hunter had finished off the whiskey days ago, his tobacco supply was getting low, and he needed a bath. Hopefully, the place he was heading for had survived the Indian wars. If not, the half-breed was in for a long week. With a full stomach of deer steak, he rode on. If his memory served, he should be close now. Hunter pictured the town in his head. He remembered a trading post, and a country store located next to a whorehouse. Across the street was a Hotel and saloon. It would be nice to sleep in a warm, dry bed for a change, and with little thought, he could taste the whiskey pouring down his throat to warm his belly.

Night was falling; suddenly there was a movement up ahead, near what appeared to be a bend in the road. Hunter pulled back the reins, halting his horse in its tracks. Listening and looking forward, he heard a creaking sound. After a short moment of study, he realized what it was. Hunter rode up to it.

The sign swinging in the wind, read:

Myakka City

Pop. 60

Well how 'bout that, he thought, puzzled. *Myakka is a city now.*

He turned the corner, moving up the road a spell before entering the small town. He dismounted in front of Mats Place Hotel Saloon. A handsome boy, who looked to be no more than ten years old, jumped down off the porch. Without saying a word, he took the reins from Hunter and turned the Appaloosa down the street, heading toward a large barn, half-painted red.

"Do you work here, boy?" asked Hunter, "Or are you the South's youngest horse thief?"

"No need to fret, Mister, I work here," replied the boy, then he continued to lead the horse away.

Satisfied he wasn't being rustled, Hunter walked in through the hanging doors of the saloon. Standing just inside the entryway, he looked around. He first noticed half a dozen men playing poker at two of the five tables, giving him a glance as he entered. Cheers erupted from some rugged looking gamblers playing craps in the far corner of the room. They were next to the stairs that led up to the second story.

Hunter recognized the elderly man behind the bar that stretched across the entire back wall. He walked over, the sound of his spurs clinking on the dirty, pinewood planked floors. He tossed a gold piece on the counter.

"Hunter James," the old man said as he served him up a glass of beer and a bottle. "Been a long time, six, maybe eight years, or so."

"Howdy, Matt. Seems more like twenty, by the looks of you."

Matt laughed louder than Hunter expected, then said, "Well, you were just a kid when you left on out of here, with three dead men under your belt, as I recall."

Two cowhands at the other end of the bar overheard this and glanced in his direction.

Hunter replied, "Yeah, well, I lost track over the years. Don't matter much; ammo's fairly easy to come by."

Hunter took a swig of his beer, and then continued, "This place hasn't changed much, 'cept for the whorehouse across the street. I see it's a hotel now."

"Yea, some rich Yankee bought it. Old man Wilson's daughters were even gittin' too old for the boys 'round here. Bad for business with no whores 'round."

"So what's the deal, Matt, you still own this shit hole?"

"Yea, I own it; bartend, keep the peace, so to speak. But I'm gittin' old, lookin' for somebody 'round here to help keep the peace for me. Someone I can trust – maybe someone like you."

Hunter downed his beer, slamming the mug on the bar, "Don't go trusting me too much. How's 'bout a room and a bath?"

Matt turned around and grabbed a key marked number 3 and tossed it to him. The gunslinger grabbed up his bottle, walked across the room, and headed up the stairs.

"Hey, Hunter," Matt yelled after him, "I got a letter here for ya, might be important." Hunter turned at the top of the stairs, looking back.

"I'll see you in the mornin', right now I need to wash and get some shut eye."

Matt shrugged his shoulders in bewilderment, about the washing part, "Suit yourself," he replied as the gunslinger turned the corner at the top of the stairs, disappearing down the hallway.

◆❖◆

Hunter woke the next morning at sun up. He always slept well on a chicken-feathered mattress, especially with the back of the chair shoved under the doorknob for an extra lock. He dressed, pulling on his black pants, black shirt, and then his razor tip boots. His left boot sheathed a six-inch boot knife. He stood and buckled on his gunbelt which cradled the two silver colored .44 Colt Walkers and double rows of cartridges all the way around. He shoved the thirteen-inch Bowie knife inside the front of the gunbelt. The sawed off double-barreled shotgun rested nicely in the custom made, side-mount, shoulder holster. He slipped into his light-colored, elk-skin, rawhide fringed jacket with inside individual pockets that held his extra shotgun shells. He picked up his rifle, and last, but not least, he put on his black hat with its rattlesnake band. He was now ready for his morning meal.

The moment he entered the hallway, he smelled the aroma of bacon in the air wafting up from downstairs. On the first floor in the saloon was a southern style breakfast being served by a large Negro woman. Hunter overheard a patron refer to her as Bessie, as he was coming down the stairs. Matt was sitting at one of the poker tables drinking coffee. In front of him was his empty breakfast plate. After a few minutes in the chow line, Hunter walked his coffee, bacon, eggs, taters, and grits over, sitting down across from his old friend.

From his inside jacket pocket, Matt pulled out a worn faded letter and slid it across the table.

Without saying a word, Hunter picked up the paper. He removed a small knife out of a sheath that was sown into the topside of his hat. He then used it to cut the rawhide string that kept the letter closed. Unfolding it, he began to read it to himself...

Dear Son,

Even though we have never met, I have thought of you as of late, as I am gitin old. When I die I leave you my cabin behind the big oak, three hundred paces off the Myakka River. It's a good cabin, It's all I got.

James Dolin

"Where did you get this, Matt?" Hunter asked, holding up the letter in his hand.

The old man looked over his coffee cup as he took a sip, then said, "Your pa gave it to me 'bout a year back, just shy a week before some trappers found his body floating in the Myakka River." Matt paused a moment before continuing, "He was gunshot in the back."

Hunter stopped chewing his meal. "Who dun it?"

"Don't know fer sure, "Matt said in a quiet voice, leaning in towards Hunter. "Your pa made a lot of enemies in his life. If I had to guess, I'd say, Frank Lugar and his boys, Jake and little Johnny. They would be first on my list."

"What happened between this Frank and my pa?" asked Hunter, as he chewed on a piece of fatback.

Matt set down his coffee and continued to talk in a hushed tone. "Your pa and Frank's brother Billy robbed trains together. They had a falling out that ended up in a gun battle right here in this very street. He shot Billy dead. Your pa might have been a faster draw than you, but I don't think so."

Hunter finished his coffee then stood up. Setting the empty cup on the table, he grabbed his rifle and went toward the front doors.

"Where you headed?" hollered Matt from his seat.

"I'm going to see my cabin," Hunter said without turning. Then he was gone, leaving the hinges creaking as the swinging saloon doors paddled back and forth.

Matt could hear the sound of his spurs clanking on the wood deck fade, as he walked further away down the front porch.

The same boy who had taken his horse to the barn the day before, jumped up and out of a hammock tied up between two palm trees.

"Get your horse, Mister?"

"Yeah, boy. Can you saddle him and bring him out to me? There'll be a gold piece in it for ya'."

"Yes sir, Mister!"

The gunslinger watched as the boy ran next door into the half-red, half-unpainted barn. The barn, in a strange way, reminded Hunter of himself. He also liked this small, good-looking boy from the beginning. The youngster seemed hard working and respectful, there weren't many like him around these parts.

Hunter stood in the street rolling a smoke in his good hand, which was a bit of a chore. His left hand used to be the quickest, but now that he was missing part of his middle finger, his right hand might temporarily be dominant.

Ten minutes or so had gone by and he started to wonder if he might need to lend a hand, when the boy appeared through the big double doors, the wind blowing his shoulder length, sandy-brown hair.

"Here's your horse, Mister."

Hunter checked the App over. He looked clean and brushed. Walking around to the other side of the horse, he loosened and then re-tightened the belly strap.

"You do good work, son; been doin' it long?"

"Yes sir, all my life," the boy said proudly.

"All your life, huh?" said Hunter with a grin. "What's your name, boy?"

"Zeke." said the boy.

"Tell me, Zeke, is there a cabin on the river by a big oak?"

"Oh, yes sir, Mister, 'bout half a day's walk south a' here. Follow the river, you can't miss it."

Hunter mounted his horse and reached into his top pocket. He plucked out a gold piece and flipped it to the boy. The boy caught the worn gold coin, and in one motion slid it into the front of his trousers.

Hunter thought, *that boy could be a gunfighter one day, with the proper training,* as he rode out of town. He headed south then west toward the river to find his cabin, and possibly his home.

Was he old enough to have shaken off that traveling urge? Was he tired enough to settle down? He didn't know. Hell, nobody knew. All he knew for sure was sooner or later he would run into the man or men that killed his pa, and he would kill them, or his name wasn't Hunter James Dolin.

CHAPTER THREE

Hunter traveled easily down the wagon trail, riding at a steady gallop. It was mid-morning and very cool for this time of year. "Whoa, boy," he said softly as he pulled back on the reins. He untied his leather-skinned water pouch and took a long drink. He looked about studying the land, some of it was familiar to him, but a lot of it had changed. He noticed the trees had grown much taller. He had traveled this same road as a small boy, when it was no more than a goat path. Today the land was more open, but somehow seemed older.

He realized he could hear rushing water to his right. Quickly tying off the pouch, he maneuvered the Appaloosa, making his own opening straight through a thin growing part of the brushy tree line. He broke out onto some grassy flatlands, one hundred feet from the river. The boy was right, you couldn't miss it. On the other side of the bank, where the water was shallow and fast moving, proudly stood the giant oak, shading the modest log cabin from the morning sun. There was also a small barn, and besides that, a corral for livestock. A hundred yards beyond was the main river.

With a kick of the spurs and a "Ya", the horse and rider took off as one, disturbing the flow of the knee-deep waters as they crossed.

All in one motion, Hunter slowed the App to a stop and dismounted in front of the cabin. He stood for a moment, combing the countryside with his eyes and ears for intruders. Satisfied there was no one about, he kicked the heavy wood door open with one boot, pistol drawn, and took a step down into the log structure. Lucky for them he was alone.

It was a small, well built, one-roomer. There was a bed with a mattress, a wood-burning stove, and a kitchen table, with two mismatched chairs. There were six windows, two in front, two in back, and one on each side. They were made of wood shutters, split down the middle with cross-shaped slits carved out at their centers. These crosses looked like religious symbols, but he knew they were portals for shooting rifles out of. Up and down, or side to side. He walked to the center of the room, studying the floor as he went – wood planked, and dug out a foot deep below the doorjamb. With a hand ax, you could easily chop out slits between the logs, lay low, and shoot your enemy outside with full cover from a belly position. The cabin had so much mud packed on it; it would be hard to burn. Only an outlaw expecting trouble would build a fortress like this._ *Yup*, he thought, *this is for sure the cabin my pa built; James Dolin is written all over this place.*

Exiting his small domain, Hunter closed the door behind him, mounted his horse, and headed back the way he came. He glanced once again at the small barn and coral, much like any other he'd seen before.

As he rode, he thought about supplies he would need to live out here in his cabin. There was no hurry, he had plenty of gold to pay for a room at the hotel, and Bessie cooked some good grub. There was gambling to be done, and it had been a long while since he smelled a woman up close. Hunter was smiling and wondering where all the pretty women were, when his horse suddenly spooked at a gunshot, coming from what seemed to be the wagon trail on the other side of the tree line.

He quietly rode through the brush onto the path. There he saw a family, a man, a woman, two girls, and a small boy in a covered wagon. Three Indians on horseback were holding them up at gunpoint. Two others had dismounted and were ransacking a pack mule tied up alongside. They were so busy with what they were doing; they didn't hear Hunter stroll up behind them.

He came to a halt, at a distance of ten feet. He quietly pulled out the shortened double-barreled shotgun and laid it over the saddle, pointing directly at their backs. With the other hand, he then pulled the shiny revolver and, with a loud boom, he shot the feathers off the head of the short, chubby Indian rummaging through the family belongings. This immediately got everyone's attention.

The featherless Indian stared in disbelief. The three on horseback turned quickly, Hunter brought up the shotgun at the same time clicking both hammers back with his thumb.

"Hold it right there," he told them. "This here scatter-gun at this distance will do some damage to you all. And this .44..." Hunter held up the revolver, spun it sideways, spun it forward, spun it backward into the holster, and back out again, aiming at the two on the ground as he cocked the trigger back with his thumb, "won't be shootin' feathers this time."

Even if these savages didn't speak English, the gunslinger knew they understood what he meant. Staring down the barrels of a sawed-off shotgun needed no translation; this language was worldwide.

The leader of this bunch said some words in Injun. The two braves on foot, doing the ransacking, jumped up on their horses and rode off into the swamp. The other two on horseback slowly followed.

The leader stared into the half-breed's eyes, possibly searching for fear. There was none. He then looked down at the shotgun, before yelling out in his best

Indian war cry while rearing up his horse, he turned and followed his braves without looking back.

The middle-aged man jumped down from the wagon, and walked over to his savior on the spotted horse.

"Thank ya, Mister; you come along in the nick of time."

Hunter replaced the .44 cartridge with a new one, before putting his guns away, then lit up a smoke.

The older man was impressed with the speed with which he did this.

"Well, I didn't like the odds much. You all headin' for town?"

"I'm Doc Harmon, this is my wife Lizzy, and these are my three children. And yes, we're tryin' to get to Myakka City."

"Well, Doc, git your goods together, and I'll ride you in the rest of the way."

"Are you the law 'round here, sir?"

"No, I'm a man like any other."

"I doubt that," said the doc with much conviction.

The gunslinger snapped his fingers several times, "Come on Doc, lets git movin', ain't safe out here in the open."

"Yes sir, thank you, sir."

They made it into town without further incident. Hunter tipped his hat to the women folk, and then rode on down toward the saloon, planning to have a chat with Matt and a drink or three. It was nearly high noon and he felt his tongue might swell with the heat.

He stabled the Appaloosa with the boy inside the barn, and began checking over his packhorse.

"Everythin' is just the way you left it, Mister," Zeke said, his head held high.

"I see that. Keep up the good work, boy, and we'll git along just fine."

After a wink and a nod to the boy, Hunter checked his guns. The gunslinger did this out of pure habit, more than anything. He then walked the dusty, horse-manure ridden road, up the steps and into the saloon. He walked through the small crowd to the far end of the bar before turning and putting his back against the wall. He struck a stick-match, bringing it up to the end of his unlit cigar. As smoke billowed out from under Hunter's hat like a chimney, Matt set a beer down in front of him. He then filled a shot glass full of his good whiskey for both of them. They stood across the bar from each other, drinking for a time, before Matt broke the silence.

"Seen you ride in with the new doc. They run across some trouble?"

"You don't miss much 'round here, do you, Matt?"

"I've learned over the years that a mere scrap of information can save your life."

"Yeah," replied Hunter, sarcastically. "I think you've also learned over the years to gossip like a church lady."

Matt chuckled at this comment, like he so often did.

Hunter finished his beer and slammed back another shot of whiskey. Matt refilled his glass, while the gunslinger continued the conversation.

"I just happened to come along on Doc and his family being held up by some renegade Indians. The lead brave was Miccosukee, I'm sure of that; he had what looked like a tomahawk scar on his left cheek." As Hunter said this, he ran his index finger from his temple down to his jaw. "I run them off without trouble, havin' them dead to rites with the scatter-gun."

"You son-of-a-bitch." Matt laughed from the gut. "You been back in these parts 'bout a month now, and you're already makin' enemies. You're a Dolin all right. That's Buffalo Tiger; he runs a small band of renegades that done been run out of the Tennessee valley a few years back, And if you made him look weak in front of his braves, he'll be lookin' to run across you again."

Hunter did not reply or show any reaction whatsoever.

"Well, what cha gonna' do, son?" asked Matt.

"Right now, I'm gonna' whip some ass at one of them there card tables." He nodded toward a couple of old cowboys starting up a game of poker; they had the look of veterans from wars past. Hunter walked over to the table, his spurs clanking.

"You boys lookin' to play some poker?"

The cowboys looked up and saw a man, six-foot-two, long jet-black hair, with steel blue eyes that pierced souls and made a man feel vulnerable. He had weapons from his cowboy hat to his razor sharp, knife-tipped boots. He was twenty-five, maybe thirty, they didn't know – hard to tell 'til you knew what a man'd been through.

One of the old veterans, with chin whiskers down to his belly, and a nine-inch scar down his throat, asked in a raspy voice.

"Are you James Dolin's Injun bastard son, the one everybody's been talkin' 'bout?"

"That'd be me," said Hunter.

The other man at the table was older as well. He was short and stocky and had an impressive handlebar mustache. Both men had hair white as snow, but Hunter could tell these two weren't far beyond their prime.

"Got any money?" asked the man with the handlebar mustache. "We ain't playin' for red cloth."

That comment got a cackle from them two. They sounded like a couple of old hens.

Hunter slowly reached into his inside coat pocket.

This stopped the cackling, and put a look of concern on their faces, until Hunter pulled out a drawstring leather satchel and tossed it on the table with a thud and a clank. "Spanish gold coin good enough for ya?" asked the gunslinger.

The two men glanced at each other and grunted just a bit. "Have a seat, maybe we can separate you from some of that Spanish treasure?"

Come to find out, from little more than small talk, the old guys Jebediah and Walt, had known and somewhat respected his pa. Maybe it was fear; he wasn't sure. Never the less, their poker game went on through the night. The games were fairly close with Hunter up from the beginning. He backed off enough hands so not to anger the old veterans. It seemed, over the few hours at the table, they developed an unspoken bond between them.

Might mean somthin' down the road, Hunter thought. *Then again, it might not. No tellin' what side a man could find himself on.*

Hunter's need to gamble was satisfied and he began thinking about sleep. He scraped up his winnings, thanked the old men for their contributions, and headed towards the stairs.

Before he reached the first step, he heard arguing coming from behind him. He turned around and walked over to his spot at the end of the bar, placing his hands palm down on top of it.

Matt and a disgruntled man were twelve feet away from him. They faced each other, the two-foot wide counter separated them.

Hunter figured the patron was a trapper by the way he was dressed. He had clothes made of otter pelts, and a coonskin cap. His rifle leaned against a chair by his side, but Hunter's main concern was the revolver he was waving around in the air. The trapper was clearly drunk and getting nastier by the minute.

Matt was speaking in a calm voice," You're cut off, sir. I suggest you go to where you come from and sleep it off."

"I ain't goin' nowheres," growled the trapper. "I want another drank, and what are you gonna' do 'bout it, huh?"

"I ain't gonna' do nothin'," Matt nodded his head in Hunter's direction, "But that man at the end of the bar will."

The trapper turned toward the gunslinger, squinting his eyes through his drunken haze. "Yeah, and who the Hell 'er you?"

"I'm the peace keeper in here," Hunter replied, his hands still palm down on the bar's countertop, "and you're disturbin' it."

The trapper looked to Matt, then back to Hunter. "Well, screw you," he said, as he brought his arm up, pistol in hand.

Hunter pulled his shiny silver colt out of his holster, faster than anyone had seen before, and blasted the trapper's gun from his mitt, shattering it into who knew how many pieces.

At that moment, Matt reached across the bar, grabbed the drunken man's rifle from its leaning position against the chair, and whacked him upside the head with it. The man hit the wood floor with a thud.

Matt yelled through the room, "Anyone know this drunken ass trapper?" Two men with coonskin caps walked up from the back of the saloon.

"We know 'im," said one. "He's with us, but we don't want no trouble."

"Well, git that son-of-a-bitch out of my saloon before I whack him in the head again."

Hunter had walked up and collected a second pistol from the sprawled out trapper's belt. He unloaded the cylinder and handed the gun to Matt who took it and stuck it behind the bar.

The two men quickly picked up their laid-out friend, hands under each arm, and began dragging him toward the door.

"I don't want to see him anymore tonight!" yelled Matt from behind the bar, "he can pick up his guns tomorrow when he sobers up." Matt turned and looked at Hunter. "Good job, son, thank ya much."

"Don't thank me. It's gonna' cost ya free room, meals, beer, oh, an' whiskey – the good whiskey."

"Well," Matt replied, a look on his face that said he'd just been had, and knew it. "I guess you've decided to work around here, and it's a deal then."

"Yup," Hunter replied as he walked toward the stairs. "I guess it is a deal then. Goodnight, Matt."

"Night, Dolin." Then under his breath, Matt grumbled, "Thievin' son-of-a-..."

◆❖◆

It was early winter. The air was unusually dry for the swamp. It had been over a week since the last rain, and the ground was already dried out from the bright Florida sun. Hunter had awoken early and dressed. After eating Bessie's southern morning meal, he went down to the country store and picked up supplies for the cabin. With the packhorse in tow, he headed south down the Myakka River trail. His Appaloosa seemed to take to the cold crisp air.

There was a mile of landscape behind him when his horse suddenly alerted him with a snort. The gunslinger sensed a presence seconds before he saw it. About a hundred feet down the path stood the scar-face warrior called Buffalo Tiger. He had a ten-inch blade clenched in his right hand. He was alone, and his face was bordered with war paint.

Great, Hunter thought, *that's all I need this mornin'.* He continued on slowly 'til he was twenty paces from the Indian. He looked around behind him and into the woods on both sides of the trail. No movement, that he could see. Content it was just the two of them, he dismounted.

"This don't hafta' to be," Hunter said simply.

The warrior said nothing, just stared with conviction.

Hunter walked his Appaloosa and the packhorse off the path a bit, wrapping the reins around the branch of a small scrub-oak. He took off his gunbelt and draped it over the saddle. Then he pulled out the shotgun from his side holster, sliding it into a vertical holder atop his rig. This scabbard was positioned where he could get to it in case his skills went south. After removing his jacket, he pulled out the Bowie knife with his right hand and moved forward.

They began circling. The Injun warrior lunged toward him, his knife in his fist in an over-hand stabbing motion. Hunter grabbed his wrist with his empty hand and barrel-rolled him over the top. They both came to their feet, separated at the same time, turning around and facing each other.

They began circling once again.

Hunter jabbed twice at the Injun's knife hand, barely missing. The warrior counter-jabbed at Hunter's face then his chest. He also missed.

I'd better put an end to this before someone gits hurt, Hunter thought; *namely me.*

Buffalo Tiger yelled out a warrior cry and lunged at Hunter, slamming his shoulder into his waist. The gunslinger took it and rolled with it onto his back, continuing over 'til he was on top of his worthy opponent. He held his knife to the Injun's throat, stopping all movement. It was over as quickly as it had begun.

With one flick of his wrist, Hunter could have ended the brave's life, but thought better of it. All he needed was the rest of Buffalo Tiger's renegades tracking him down. He took the Miccosukee's knife from him, before taking the blade from his neck.

Hunter stood up and walked to his horse. He kept a close eye on the Indian while strapping on his gear.

Buffalo Tiger got to his feet and walked to the edge of the woods, and then turned, staring at the half-breed gunslinger.

Hunter gave him a nod of respect then tossed him his knife, which the Indian caught without batting an eye, slipping it into his waist flap. After a slight pause, the scar-faced warrior disappeared into the swamp.

Hunter slid his foot in the stirrup, slinging his other leg over. He continued on, while talking aloud to his horse, "I think we should try stayin' off this damn road, too many Indians travelin' it. What do ya think?"

As if he understood, the Appaloosa shook his head and whinnied.

"Come on, boy. Let's see if we can get where we're goin' without any more troubles."

At a steady gallop, they made it to the cabin in no time at all. After checking the cabin for unwanted guests, Hunter unloaded the packhorse and put the goods in their proper places. He removed the App's saddle and brushed down both horses from head to hoof. He made several trips back and forth from the river with buckets, one in each hand, until the water trough was full. He dumped half a bag of grain into a smaller trough, and left the animals safely corralled for the night. The gunslinger went inside and pan fried a deer steak on the wood stove, ate it, and then retired to the small front porch to watch the sunset with a smoke.

As the sun went down, and the whippoorwills began to whip-poor-will, he thought, *I could git used to this kind of livin'. But to settle down here, I would need a strong handsome woman to share it with. And where is there a good woman way the hell out here? Damn, I must be gittin' old, thinkin' thoughts like this.*

He took a swig off a whiskey bottle as he watched a paddleboat go down the main part of the river, its large stacks pouring out steam. He wondered if this could be the beginning of a new way of life for him, or just a lull in the old one. Was he going stupid? *A wife, always nagging with, You're drinking too much, stop gambling, when are you coming home? Am I pretty? Christ,* he thought, *he didn't need that. Besides, there weren't any marryin' kind 'round here anyhow.*

He drank the bottle dry, dropping it to the wood porch while stumbling through the door of the cabin. Spurred by habit, he grabbed a chair and shoved it under the door handle. The drunk gunslinger stumbled over to his bed and passed out face first, guns still strapped on, and all. Only good luck kept him from shooting himself in his stupor.

♦❖♦

For the next couple of weeks, Hunter spent half his time at the cabin and the other half at Matt's place. The cabin roof needed some fixing, so he did a little roof patch, made up of mud and hay. He fixed the corral fence that had some termite damage. With the packhorse turned mule, he hired Zeke the stable boy to do some log collecting for replacing a fence post here and there.

Before any of this handy work took place, Hunter was compelled, for no reason he knew at the time, to dig out the gun shooting slits near the cabin floor. He thought maybe he was just in survival mode, or maybe in the back of his mind he knew, for him, trouble was always right around the bend.

It was refreshing to be doing honest, hard work on his own land. It was also just plain fun being down at the saloon, getting drunk with Matt, playing poker, and keeping the peace. Kicking ass when the cowboys and trappers got out of hand was part of his job; Hunter thought of it as sort of a bonus. Life was good, life was simple, but unbeknownst to him, life was going to get very, very complicated, very, very quickly.

CHAPTER FOUR

She arrived by stagecoach in front of the Jackson Hotel located across the street from Matt's Place. The Jackson stood where Wilson's whorehouse used to be. Bigger and newer than Matt's by a decade, it looked out of place here in Myakka. As far as Hunter could tell, the place had been empty since he came to town. Without gambling or whores, there was no reason for the men of these parts to even pass through the doors. This place was just another rich Yankee's winter home, which was becoming more common every other day in this southern state.

It was early evening, the rainy weather was gone for now, the weather was warmer than since the gunslinger had arrived. Mosquitoes buzzed their ears regularly. Hunter and Matt sat in rocking chairs on the saloon's front porch, smoking cigars, and getting some fresh air, when a stagecoach pulled up. The stagehand who rode shotgun jumped down and opened the door.

Out stepped the most beautiful woman Hunter had ever seen. The sun was setting just above the tree line, but was still bright enough to light up her long auburn hair. She was wearing a low cut, tight, cream-colored dress which she filled out nicely. Hunter stopped rocking his chair, staring in amazement.

Matt's lit cigar dropped out of his open mouth and fell into his lap, causing sparks to fly everywhere. He was trying to stand, arms a flailing, the hot cherry breaking up into many smaller embers burning him and Hunter.

"Damn, Matt!" Hunter yelled as he stood, while trying to put out the small fires on his shirt and britches.

"Sorry 'bout that, son; but *damn*, there goes the neighborhood. A woman like that 'round here ain't nothin' but trouble."

They stopped bickering at each other for a moment and raised their heads. The woman was looking, smiling right at them. They clumsily removed their hats.

She nodded with a small curtsy and headed up the steps, then disappeared through the front doors of the hotel.

"Who is she, Matt?" Hunter asked.

"I dunno, son. Ain't ever seen her before."

By this time, a small crowd had formed here and there. Hunter spotted Zeke and began waving at him, "Come on over here, boy."

The boy ran up. "Yes, sir."

Hunter still wasn't used to how polite this young man was. He liked him more and more each day. He flipped him a gold piece and followed up with instructions.

"Zeke, without causin' attention to yourself, find out everythin' about that lady that you can. All right?"

With a 'cat that ate the bird' grin on his face, the boy ran off toward the hotel.

"You're really takin' a likin' to that boy ain't ya?" commented Matt.

"That little shit's got half my gold stash," Hunter replied, an annoyed look on his face. "Hell, he's gonna' own this town someday."

"Yup, whatever you say, Mr. Dolin."

"The hell with this," Hunter mumbled as he walked into the saloon. "I need a drink."

He bellied up to the bar and got a beer from Jimmy, one of Matt's bartenders. He was an older man, a local

Matt grew up with. He was a man Matt would say he trusted.

"Jimmy, give me a bottle and a beer, would ya?"

"Matt told me to give you whatever you asked fer," Jimmy said, as he set a glass full of draft and a bottle of whiskey on the counter.

Hunter emptied his beer in one gulp. "Damn, must be a hole in the bottom," he said while staring into the glass. He snatched up the whiskey bottle by the neck and retreated to a small table in the corner. He sat down on the wobbly wood chair with his back against the wall and took a long swig. He wondered why he was so testy. Was it the fact that he had father-like feelings for Zeke? Or because he had a schoolboy crush on a woman he saw for two minutes? She was so beautiful. The problem was, settling down in one place around these people was making him weak. Being on the trail, traveling through the woods, keeps a man close to nature and God; it keeps a man's wits about him. Having relations with people makes life much more complicated. He was still young, and now he was seeking family life; something he'd never had before.

He took another long draw off the bottle. *Christ*, he thought, *now I'm soundin' like a tenderfoot. Next, I'll be cryin' like a woman.*

Suddenly, as if on cue, a fight broke out at one of the poker tables near the other end of the bar, ending Hunter's emotional thoughts. He stood and walked across the room without breaking a stride, and began beating on the two tussling cowhands. He pulled them apart and stepped in between them. He punched one in the mouth with a right jab, then coming back with his right elbow struck the other man's nose.

Blood splattered in all directions as one man fell on his back one way while the other man fell on his back the other, smashing two chairs and a table. Both men quickly began to rise, hands on their side-arms, ready to draw. Before they could get past a crouching position, they were met with Hunter's Walker Colt gun barrels to their foreheads, stopping all movement.

"Are you boys done?" Hunter said sternly. "Give me a reason, and I'll splatter your brains all over these walls."

By this time, Matt heard the commotion. He came in from the front porch through the swinging doors to see Hunter, who looked to him like a giant eagle with silver colts at the end of each wing. From the bottom of each outstretched arm, the rawhide tassels hung down like feathers.

The cowboys' eyes were as wide as they could get. They both took their hands off their guns and raised their arms slowly at the same time. These two also looked like birds to Matt, but not eagles; they looked more like prey.

They backed up from those shiny pistols and scurried out the front door as Hunter twirled his revolvers, spinning them back into their holsters. Feeling like a man again, he walked to his table, grabbed the half-empty whiskey bottle, and headed up the stairs. He would not gamble tonight, he wasn't in the mood.

"G'night, Matt."

"Night, gunslinger."

◆❖◆

Hunter awoke early the next morning, as usual; he combed his hair and washed his teeth with his forefinger and some lard soap. He dressed, strapped on his weapons, and removed the chair from under the door, before heading down the stairs.

Matt was sitting at his favorite poker table drinking his coffee and reading the oldest looking Bible Hunter had ever seen. It dawned on him, it must be Sunday. Bessie was dishing out vittles to several cowboys, while Zeke was running in and out with a bucket of water for the cleaning of the dishes. Hunter sat down across from Matt at his table.

"Mornin', Matt."

"Mornin', son," replied Matt, without looking up from his Holy book.

At that moment, Bessie brought over two plates of food and poured coffee.

"Thanks, Bess," Hunter offered with a small grin and a nod.

"Yessum, Mr. Dolin," replied Bessie, without making eye contact.

"Please call me Hunter."

"Yessum, Mr. Hunter," Bessie said as she scampered away to attend to other hungry patrons. Hunter stared at Matt for a few seconds trying to get his attention, to no avail.

"Why is she so jumpy around me?"

Matt stopped reading and set down his book, and then he began counting off on his fingers: "Number **one**, she's a black woman livin' in the south, which I would consider at this day and age unstable territory; number two, she knew your pa, he was a hard man in these parts who was known for his mean streak."

Hunter continued looking up at Matt from his breakfast, not saying anything.

Matt continued, "And number three, he could be an intimidatin' son-of-a-gun. Your pa was one of few men that didn't have no weak nerve." Matt took a bite of his eggs, and washed it down with his coffee. He leaned back in his creaky wooden chair and finished his thought, "He did have a good side; he just didn't show it off much."

Hunter pondered this for a moment. "All right, let me get this straight. Bessie was born a poor black child, my old man was scary, and she thinks the apple doesn't fall far from the tree. Does that about sum it up?"

"I reckon," said Matt.

They finished their vittles in silence. This early the saloon was fairly quiet except for some cattlemen and a few farmers in town for supplies and whatnot. Hunter was lighting up a smoke when Zeke ducked under the saloon doors and walked up to their table, his hat in hand.

"What can I do for you, son?" asked Hunter.

"I have some news on that lady, Mister."

"Well, let's hear what you got," replied Hunter, puffing on his newly rolled cigar.

The boy stood at attention like a little soldier and spoke quietly. "Her name is Lilith Montgomery. She's the daughter of Richard Montgomery, a gold miner that struck it rich in Denver, Colorado. She was sent down here by her father, for her safety, 'cause of the war brewin' between the states. That's all I heard this time."

"Thank ya, son. Run along now, but let me know if you hear more."

"Yes sir," Zeke said as he ran off, ducking back under the front swinging doors, the same way he had entered.

Hunter pushed his empty plate to the middle of the table with a sigh. He struck a match on the table and relit his cigar that had gone out. *This tobacco is too wet, I need to lay them in the sun for a bit,* thought Hunter.

A long silence was broken when the gunslinger made a comment, followed by a question, "This war between the states is gonna' be a bad one, Matt. A lot of Americans will die, and there doesn't look to be any way around it. What do you think?"

"Yup, this war is gonna' divide families right down the middle, brother against brother, father against son."

There was a pause as they both blew out smoke, then Hunter asked Matt, "Where do you stand on the slavery issue?"

"Well, I see it this way, people fled England to be free in America, so how is it right to have slaves of any kind in this country? But, then again, I also understand men fightin' for a way of life that's been goin' on for a hundred years. Make no mistake, this war isn't just about slavery, it's about power and government." Matt paused for a moment then leaned in closer toward Hunter.

"These swamps in this Florida peninsula is gonna' possibly be a safe haven for deserters, slaves, renegade Indians, and anyone else who wants to stay out of the bloodshed. That could be good for business."

"Well, I tend to agree with you, Matt, for the most part, but where there's more people, there's more trouble."

Matt put his hands up in the air. "Well, that's what I have you here for, Hunter James."

"I reckon so," said Hunter with a smile, stood, and shuffled on out of the building. He stood on the front steps of Matt's place with the now unlit stub of a cigar between his teeth. He was wondering if it was too early for a beer, when he heard the crack of the whips and the beating hooves of running cattle. The sound was off in the distance, but getting closer from the North. *The crackers were coming.*

He hurriedly walked around to the back of the saloon, where they came out of a cloud of dust. There must have been, he figured, at least a thousand head of cattle. They were twenty or so wide, and fifty or sixty deep. There were cowboys with bullwhips up front, on the sides, and toward the back, six, maybe eight, total. They all had bandanas tied around their nose and mouth to keep the dirt cloud out. They looked like grimy bank robbers.

He spotted several black mouth curs, these were cowherding dogs, and they were moving them quick, picking up the slack between the gaps. The herd's numbers were great, taking them several minutes to pass.

The crackers were getting close to home and they

were on the downhill side of their long journey. They didn't notice Hunter standing there, watching them, until the last rider at the back rolled up. Even with a bandana over his face, and his body covered with dust, Hunter sensed he was the elder and the leader of these men.

The older, dusty man pulled on the reins, the horse stopped and reared. The horse did a 360 degree turn, and reared again, then settled down on all four hooves.

Their eyes met for a moment. Hunter saw the face of a man who had just seen a ghost. Then those eyes suddenly narrowed to a look of cold heartlessness. The drover's legs kicked, spurring the horse into action, and he took off after the dust cloud of the diminishing cattle.

Hunter heard a boot shuffle behind him to his left. With lightning speed, he pulled his pistols simultaneously as he spun around, hammers cocked.

There stood Matt, staring down Hunter's two gun barrels, eyes wide open, and his hands palm out.

"Easy simmer, easy simmer, son! It's just me."

"Damn it, Matt, don't sneak up on me like that! You tryin' to get yourself killed?"

The gunslinger twirled his guns back into their holsters, and took a deep breath. He felt like he had forgotten to breathe for a while.

"Who was that, Matt?"

"That was Frank Lugar. In a day or so, him and his men will be hittin' town, gittin' drunk, and lookin' for trouble. Maybe you should go hang out at that cabin of yours for a while."

Hunter walked up to Matt, put his arm around him, and steered him toward the front of the saloon. "Come on, old man. If there's trouble brewin' in a few days, then we better get drunk this day."

Matt replied with a smile, "Well, if you're gonna' arm twist, why the hell not?"

CHAPTER FIVE

Frank Lugar and his boys had been running cattle for many weeks. They were finally home, corralling the herd on three, maybe as much as four hundred acres known to the locals as Lugar's Ranch.

Florida was an open range, but Frank spent some time in Texas and knew the advantages of holding and branding cattle. His ranch was the first fenced pasture in the state.

During the summer months, the herds grazed on the green luscious grasses in north Florida, up near the Georgia border. In the winter months, they would bring the cattle back home to Myakka, away from the cold and onto better grazing.

Lugar's ranch was impressive, completely fenced off with a hundred acres in the back, two hundred acres on the sides and the front, all surrounding the main house. There was cross-fencing around grazing areas, with patches of cypress forests throughout. At the entrance, a large wood-burned sign hung from a log beam supported by log posts and held up by rusty chains. It read Big L Ranch. The twenty-foot wide dirt road stretching to the two-story house was an eighth of a mile long. To the left of the house, facing east was a large red barn. The bunkhouse was on the west side where the working hands of the ranch bedded down during the night. The five room, two-story house was where Frank and his two boys lived.

Their momma had passed long ago; she had died at Johnny's birth. In the back of Frank's mind, he blamed Johnny for his wife's death. Frank would beat little Johnny on occasion when he drank too much; this was just the way it was.

Frank and his boys were already cleaned up and waiting on supper at the kitchen table, when the big man named Gator, entered through the side door.

He was Frank's number one. Gator was six-foot-four, weighed two hundred-sixty-five pounds, and was as ferocious as a grizzly bear with an attitude. His mother and father disappeared when he was ten, and he had raised himself in the swamps. Some said he killed his parents out of pure meanness, but no one knew for sure, and no one dared to ask.

Gator had to duck under the doorjamb as he entered the room.

"Mr. Lugar, all the cattle are out to pasture. The boys are eatin' stew that the Chinaman brung um. We'll be turnin' in, if you don't need us no mores."

The Chinaman's name was Chinn Yang; he cooked at the ranch, did the wash, and anything else Frank Lugar told him to. He was, after all, Frank's property – bought and paid for.

"Yeah, Gator, you get some grub, turn in. At sunup, I want two big long-horned cracker cows slaughtered and cooked for the men out there. I want them to get a proper meal, and then we'll go from there."

"Yessir," said Gator, then he ducked on his way out through a different door at the back of the kitchen.

Chinn entered from the cooking area with three bowls, wood spoons, and a big pot of stew. Jake and little Johnny were already seated at the table on one side, Frank sat down on the other. Chinn Yang scooped out the three bowls of beef and potato soup. He then set the pot on the table next to two bottles of whiskey and three glasses he'd put there earlier.

The Lugers ate and drank in silence, except for the lip smacking and belching, until Frank remembered a question he was meaning to ask.

"Did you boys see the man standin' behind Matt's place when we run the herd through the back of town?"

"No, sir, I didn't see no one," said little Johnny.

Frank looked at Jake. "What about you?"

"No sir; I couldn't see nothin'. Hell, my eyes were caked with road dust."

"Who'd you see, pa?" asked little Johnny.

Frank had to swallow a big chunk of stew meat before he could answer Johnny's question. "At first glance, I saw a long haired half-breed, and then I looked into his eyes and thought I seen James Dolin starin' back at me."

"Shit!" said little Johnny, eyes and mouth wide open expressing his shock and fear.

"Then I reckoned it must be his boy, Hunter."

Jake took a swig off the bottle wiping his mouth with his shirtsleeve, before asking a troubling question. "Do you think he knows, Pa?"

"I bet hell or high water that old jackass Matt told him what most people suspect 'round here, that we killed him."

Jake pushed his plate to the middle of the table, looking like he just lost his appetite.

"You know, pa, Hunter Dolin was seen with Huey and his crew at the Cracker Saloon, three days before we found them gutted and shot on the back trail. They—"

Little Johnny perked up, interrupting Jake. "Well, that means we're even then, right, pa?"

"No, dummy, he killed men that worked for me. We shot his old man in the back. Means we ain't even, not in his mind, 'til he kills us. He's part savage, and you know 'bout them."

"What do we do?" asked Jake.

Frank leaned back in his chair, and took a swig off the whiskey bottle he'd been holding in his hand.

"Tomorrow night we'll take Gator and some of the boys to Matt's for some drinkin'. We'll find out what that half-breed's up to. Now let's eat up, get some rest; we got another long day tomorrow."

◆❖◆

A cold front came through the panhandle that night, and the northern dry air temporarily beat down the southern swamp's constant flow of humidity. The next morning was a chilly 49 degrees. The sun rose slowly through the pine trees, bright, glaring, and yellow. The seagulls and turkey buzzards circled up in the sky, intertwined together, searching for their next meal.

A beautiful start to a beautiful day except for the commotion coming from the fourth floor of the Jackson Hotel. There was yelling, followed by broken glass, and a woman's voice carrying through the cold crisp air.

"Stay away from me, you heartless jackal! I told you never again! I'm through with you!"

"Know your place woman!" boomed a man's voice in reply.

Hunter had just pulled his head up out of the horse's watering trough when he heard a woman's scream, and once again the sound of shattering glass. Hangover and all, Hunter ran across the dirt road and through the doors of the hotel where he was confronted by two large, armed men.

Like the trees flow when the wind blows, he put a right upper cut to the left man's ribs, and with his right foot, Hunter snapped the knee of the man on his right. He then showed the man on the left more attention by grabbing the back of his head with both hands and introducing his face to a left knee, shattering his jawbone.

Hunter recovered quickly, straightened his hat, and headed toward the staircase. He had both hands on the rails, ready to catapult himself upward, when he saw her, standing halfway down the steps.

She looked even more beautiful than she had a few days ago. She wore a lovely, low-cut, green dress that seemed to be made of silk. Her breasts were heaving, and her neck was slender and graceful. They were ten-feet apart, staring at each other; it was only for a moment, but seemed like an eternity. Finally, Hunter was able to muster a question.

"Are you okay, ma'am?" he asked, gazing up from the bottom of the staircase.

"Sir, I am nineteen years old, I'm hardly a ma'am," said she, clearly with some disgust.

"All right," *Bitch,* thought Hunter. "I did not mean to offend. Are you all right, *my lady?*"

"That's better. I'm fine. I am just having a discussion with my father, Richard Montgomery. And if you don't want to be hurt, you must leave these premises immediately."

With a slight grin, Hunter turned and pointed toward the floor of the foyer. "You mean hurt, like those two? Looks like they're layin' down on the job."

"Well, we have more men," she replied in her most uppity voice.

"Is that right, *Ma'am?*" he returned with a bit of condescension of his own.

"Yes that's right, *Mister...?*"

"Hunter James Dolin," he replied, "And I hope, for your sake, your father's other men are tougher than them two."

"I assure you, Mr. Dolin—"

At that moment, Richard Montgomery walked down the stairs to Lilith's side, and put his arm around her shoulders. "Who is this man that cannot seem to mind his own business?"

"He calls himself Hunter; a savage sort of name, don't you think, father?"

Hunter stared at them for a moment through his bloodshot eyes. *Yeah, I can see were this is goin'*, Hunter thought to himself, *nowhere good.*

He turned on his heel, stepped over and around the two men groaning on the foyer floor, and exited out the front doors without looking back.

Calm and serene when he walked out of the Jackson Hotel, it took approximately ten steps into the horse dung, ridden road before he became furious. He walked up to the first cowboy he saw and clocked him right in the jaw. The man went down face first in the dirt, losing consciousness.

Before he came across any more innocent victims, Matt showed up out of nowhere and swooped Hunter up, grabbing him by the arm.

"What the hell are you doin', son?" Matt asked in what he thought was his best fatherly demeanor.

"I'm pissed off! What the hell does it look like? Now let go of me!"

Matt let go immediately – when a Dolin tells you to let go, you let go, or you might never touch anyone again.

Meeting up with his horse, Hunter unwound the reins from the hitching post, spun the Appaloosa, and mounted. He looked back over his shoulder to Matt.

"I'm goin' to the cabin, old man, before someone gets hurt."

In a cloud of dust, the gunslinger and his eager steed sped south out of town. He gave his horse his head, galloping down the road 'til he could feel the solitude radiating from the swamps around him.

He slowed the App to a walk, thinking silently, *What the hell am I doin' here, livin' amongst these people? What am I searchin' for?*

A loner for most of his life, living off the land, he was more like an Indian than a white man. Now the white man in him was taking over like a disease. After all, he was more his father as a man than like his Indian mother, a woman. He must make a choice about the war brewing inside of him.

At that moment, Hunter made a decision. He would live like a white man, for his father was a white man; and his mother was just a warm body for his father on a cold night. Life was cruel, and then some. It was now settled. He would make the cabin his home.

CHAPTER SIX

Hunter settled in for a stay. He caught small fish with a hook and line baited with rattlesnake meat, and relined bigger rigs with the small fish, catching bigger ones. He hunted the long grasses for pheasant, and used the wing-bones tied to a long raw hide line to lure the blue crabs in close, to be gigged with a stick sharpened to a point. Hunter James Dolin was living the life. He had plenty of food, whiskey, and tobacco.

It had been five, maybe six days since his little incident with the Montgomery family, and everything was hunky-dory. Then Frank and his men showed up for a chat. They rode in on their horses quickly from the southeast, catching Hunter down by the riverbank. He was wearing his Colts and his Bowie knife was tucked in his belt, but his rifle and shotgun were carelessly left up at the cabin. Hunter heard them a little way off, but he didn't have enough time to react; besides he was feeling serene this morning, and really didn't give a shit.

They lined up behind him, the five of them in a row. Hunter slowly dropped his crab line, picked up his legs from the downed cypress log he was seated on, and spun around on his backside 'til he faced the gunmen. His thumbs were hooked in the front of his belt, putting his hands inches away from his loaded Colt Walkers. He stared at Frank for a moment, and then went down the line, left to right, staring into the eyes of each man on horseback, one at a time.

They weren't scared, but they were waiting for orders. Hunter especially noticed a huge man at the end who had crazy eyes. He figured him to make the first move, if things went bad.

Hunter looked back to Frank. "You all are trespassin' on Dolin land."

Most of the five grinned and looked towards Frank, who never took his eyes off Hunter James Dolin's hands. Frank knew how dangerous this man was.

"Me and the boys here came by Matt's place the other night to give our condolences to you, for your father's accidental death."

"My father was shot in the back. I wouldn't call that an accident."

Frank paused for a time, apparently sizing up his opponent.

"Well, there's renegade Indians, fools, and outlaws in these parts, lots a' accidents can happen," explained Frank.

Hunter stood, and took a step forward.

"You're talkin' like a lawyer, Frank. Good thing for men like you and me, this town don't have no courtroom, or any law for that matter."

"What are you doin' back here in these parts, halfbreed?" asked Frank.

"My father left this land to me. I plan to settle down here. You got a problem with that, Frank?"

"No, son, as long as you doesn't interfer' with my business. I don't run the town, yet, but I sure run the lands around it."

Hunter didn't reply. He just stood there with his thumbs in his belt, with his back facing the river, carefully watching these men for the slightest movement.

Frank continued, "Hell, son, maybe we could be friends. Maybe you could work for me. I could always use another good gunman. I don't give a care that you're part Injun. Gator down there..." Frank pointed down to the end of the line. "...Hell, nobody even knows what he is."

Hunter paused in thought, *This son-of-a-bitch is as clever as a fox and as trustworthy as a snake.*

"You ought to be a politician, Frank."

Frank laughed out loud and his men laughed along with him.

Hunter continued, "In case you don't know, I'm not the friendly type. Gamblin' is my work now, and I'm not your son."

Frank sat up high in the saddle and glared into Hunter's eyes, a look that scared most men.

"Don't be a smart ass to me, boy. It's five against one. You're not that fast."

Hunter returned the glare, slowly pulled his thumbs out of his belt, sliding his hands, palms down, and rested them on his thighs. Frank's men tensed up, looking unsure about what might be happening.

"You might be right about that, Frank. I can't git you all, but I know I'll git you first."

Suddenly, unease filled the air for a moment, until Frank loosened it up a bit with a smile. "You say you're a gambler, son, and I don't think you're bluffin'. Come on boys, we got work to do."

Frank turned and rode off, his men followed. They were gone as fast as they had arrived.

Hunter walked quickly to the house and went through the door, shoulder first, grabbing the loaded rifle and his shotgun. He stepped back out onto the porch, ready for anything. There was no sign of Frank and his men, they had moved on. He sat down in his rocking chair, and looked down around his feet. He picked up a bottle of whiskey, left there from the night before, and took a long draw.

He thought about what just happened. *Never leave the cabin without the shotgun and rifle. That was a mistake; a mistake that could have been my last.*

All of a sudden, worry came over him. He needed to get to town and make sure Matt was okay.

He strapped on the rest of his gear, saddled the Appaloosa, and headed out with a strong urgency. The horse, after standing idle for too long, seemed happy to have weight on his back once again.

Hunter arrived in town as the sun reached a little past straight up, and rode straight to the saloon. He tethered his horse to the post out front, and entered through the swinging doors. A feeling of relief came over him as he saw Matt standing behind the bar. Everything looked normal. There were men strewn about, drinking and playing poker, just like any other day.

Before the gunslinger could get across the saloon floor, Matt had already poured him a beer and a shot. Hunter looked around the room once more. Satisfied there was no threat, he walked up to the bar, tossed back the whiskey, and tipped the beer back, emptying the mug, and belching loudly afterwards.

"Thanks, barkeep."

"You welcome, son. Nice to see you in one piece," Matt replied as he began drying glasses with a not so clean looking rag.

"I heard Frank and his boys come in here the other night, any trouble?"

"Just the usual – broken chairs, busted glasses, and they didn't pay for nothin'. Frank asked a few questions about you, I didn't tell him nothin." With that same dirty rag, Matt began wiping down the bar.

"Well, they figured out where I was," explained Hunter. "They paid me a little visit this mornin' at the cabin. After our chat, I know fer sure they murdered my pa, and I'll get them when the time comes."

The old bartender stopped wiping. "You be careful, son. That's a mean bunch. Other than Frank, you need to watch the one they call Gator. He's a big mean son-of-a-nobody-knows-what, raised in the swamps.

They say his parents were gators and snakes. He might be Cajun, might be Indian, or both. No one knows for sure."

Hunter nodded, "Yup, I noticed him right off; he had crazy eyes. I'll need to take him down alone, one on one, if I can."

"Why don't you just ride out a' here before the shit hits the barn door? Save yourself some trouble."

Hunter was shaking his head, east to west. "Nope, old man, I don't run. I'm gonna' live here, or I'm gonna' die right here. I'm tired of talkin' and I'm sure tired of this subject. Get me another beer, would ya?"

Matt poured him another beer, then walked to the end of the bar and refilled some other patron's empty shot glasses with whiskey. Clearly, the gunslinger was done with the run talk, and Matt knew when to excuse himself from a conversation. The old man was born at night, but it weren't last night.

Hunter was looking around for a poker game to get in on, when she walked in. His back was to the door, but he smelled her perfume before he even turned.

Some of the boys in the saloon began to hoot and holler.

"Settle down, boys!" Matt yelled out. "This here's a lady present."

Hunter turned his head back around toward the bar and began to drink his beer, trying to show little interest. It didn't work. She looked around, spotted him, and walked over to his side.

"Your name is Hunter, is it not?"

Hunter looked up with a grin. "Yes, *ma'am*."

"Please..." She smiled, even though she knew he was provoking her. "Call me Lilith."

"Well, Lilith, you shouldn't be in here. This joint ain't as high class as your father's place. What's his name again? Oh yeah, Dick!"

"His name is Richard Montgomery. But that doesn't matter for he has left town on business. I would like to hire you to escort me."

Hunter slapped a shot of whiskey back. "First of all," he said, "I'm not a babysitter, and second, why don't you get some of your father's men to take you where you want to go?"

"Most of my father's men went with him. Besides, I need someone who knows his way around these parts." As Lilith said this, she moved in closer to him. He could really smell this woman now, up close.

"And where in these parts would you like to go, Lilith?"

"I would much like to go shopping."

"Shoppin'! I got news for you, lady, this ain't Paris, or New York, this is Myakka, Florida, home of the swamp."

"*Mister* Dolin, I'm well aware what town I'm in. I would like to go to the Seminole Indian trading post. I hear they have wonderful trinkets for trade or sale."

Hunter took a sip of his beer and thought to himself, *How crazy am I, for even thinkin' of doin' this? If her father finds out, there'll be guns blazin' in the streets.* But she was so beautiful; he knew he couldn't say no.

"Okay, ma'am, but it's too late in the day. I'll take you to the post tomorrow. The roads we would be travelin' are treacherous, day or night. As a matter of fact, there's a particular stretch I always seem to have trouble on."

Lilith was shaking her beautiful head, "We will go at the bottom of the hour."

"Ma'am, you don't get it. We can't get there, trade, and get back before dark sets in. Besides—"

Lilith cut him off in mid-sentence. "I don't want to come back to town. We will stay at your cabin – it's along the way, is it not?"

Hunter's jaw dropped, "How the hell do you know...?"

"Well, it's settled then. I'll have the stable boy prepare my horse, and stop calling me *ma'am*," insisted Lilith as she turned and walked out the saloon doors.

Matt was standing halfway down the bar, just in earshot, and had been for most of the conversation. He shuffled back down across from Hunter, who was still staring at the swinging doors with his mouth hanging wide open.

"You might want to put your lips together, son," Matt chuckled, "before some flies set up camp in there."

"What the hell, old man? Were you listenin' in on mine and the lady's private talk?"

Matt was still chuckling. "Well, sure I was. I learned it from a church lady. Besides, this is my place, ain't it?"

"Yeah, it's your place all right. Don't you think it's better me gittin' a real job out there than bein' in here takin' all your patron's money at the poker tables?"

"You just do what you got to do, son, while you're still young enough to do it," Matt said with a smile. Then his look changed to serious. "You just make sure your guns are cleaned and loaded in case Montgomery finds out." *Yeah*, Matt thought to himself, *like no one ever finds out what anyone does around here.*

Without another word, Hunter stood up and began checking his guns, once again, purely out of habit, before he walked out.

He stood on the saloon's front porch surveying the streets. He kept looking over to the barn doors, waiting for her to appear. He pulled out his last large cigar from the left outside pocket of his elk-skin coat. *I need to roll some more,* he thought. He flipped the cigar into his mouth by smacking the palm of his hand with the other, in an upward motion and catching it between his teeth. He went into the right inside pocket of his jacket, moving around his smaller cigarillos 'til he found a match. Striking it on the bottom of his thigh, the match head came alive with a flash, the smell of sulfur taking over the air as he lit his smoke. *Where the hell is she?* he wondered. Who was he kidding? He would wait on this woman all day, if need be.

He was about to step down onto the street and head toward the barn, when she appeared from the doors and rode up to him sidesaddle, on the most beautiful black stallion he'd ever seen. She wore a light brown dress that came down to her ankles, with a matching cowgirl hat, and her long auburn hair pony-tailed down past the middle of her back. With his eyes, he traced the outline of her tightly worn outfit. The spell he was under was only broken by her Spencer rifle, the headstock sticking out from the saddle's sheath.

"Are you ready to go, Mr. Dolin?" she asked, followed by a big smile.

"I'm ready. I hope you can handle that animal in case we run into trouble."

"Yes, I can handle him." At that moment, she flipped her left leg over the stallion, out of her sidesaddle position, and with her foot sliding into the stirrup, she took off, the horse's hooves kicking up dirt and dust.

Hunter, staring in disbelief, jumped on his horse and took off after her. *That's one lucky saddle,* he thought to himself.

He caught up with Lilith and the black, just outside of town. They rode their horses at a walk, side-by-side for a few minutes in silence.

Until finally, Hunter had to ask, "How do you ride like that?"

"Why...whatever do you mean?" asked Lilith.

"Like a man, not side saddle?"

She looked at him with a smile, and slowly, seductively, she reached down and grabbed the bottom of her ankle-length dress. She slowly pulled upward to expose her right leg.

Hunter's eyes widened with excitement at what he might see; he then laughed a little. *Clever girl,* he thought. To his surprise, she wore a pair of man pants under her dress. Hunter had seen women in dresses, and out of dresses, but never in man pants.

"We better git movin' if we're gonna' get any shoppin' in today."

"All right," she replied, "Let's ride."

They kicked the horses in the side with their heels, and rode off down the wagon trail, heading slightly north toward the Seminole Indian trading post.

They arrived at the post with only a little time to shop before dark. They tied their horses to the hitching post, and walked down the aisles set in rows like cornfields.

These Seminole Indians were descendants of the Lower Creeks, together with remnants of the Choctaw, and other conquered tribes. Also mixed in was a large negro element of run-away slaves. It seemed to Hunter, these Indians might survive here in the swamps, unlike a lot of the other tribes out in the mid-west. The blue coats had killed or relocated the majority of the tribes that would not relent, but now were content to leave the rest alone, as a war between the states approached. If America was the melting pot of the world, then Florida was the melting pot of America.

They strolled up and down the aisles. Lilith bought some beads and a basket with, what appeared to Hunter, little enthusiasm. He felt she was just going through the motions, killing time until they must go. He had been painfully attracted to this woman ever since the first time he saw her, stepping down from the stagecoach, and then again on the stairs at the hotel. He was beginning to think she was feeling the same way toward him.

They continued along, side-by-side, not saying too much, until Hunter spoke, "Is this market what you were lookin' for?"

"Yes, it's quite nice." She stopped walking and turned to face him, taking both his hands in hers. "It's not the shopping I'm enjoying, it's the company."

Hunter was mesmerized, staring into her beautiful green eyes. They kissed slowly and passionately, her lips soft as rose petals. Hunter was thinking, *Her lips feel soft as the underbelly of a baby water moccasin.* After a moment, they pulled away from each other.

"We better head back to the cabin before it gets dark," Hunter said quietly, nervously looking around, then back to her.

"Whatever you say, Mister." Lilith replied breathlessly.

Their eye to eye contact was broken again by Hunter, who suddenly realized what they had done. Kissed in public. He glanced around once more through the small crowd, and noticed two local cowboys he knew as gamblers from Matt's saloon.

They were watching Hunter and Lilith from a distance. Men like Richard Montgomery would pay well for information, especially of this sort, and Hunter had won quite a few pots at the poker tables at the expense of those two. They could be looking to recoup some of that money.

"C'mon," Hunter said, as he lightly grabbed her arm. "Let's git outta' here," as he lead her out of the market to their horses.

They quickly mounted and headed south toward the cabin just as the sun was dropping over the tree line to the west. They rode with purpose, staying off the main trail as much as possible. They crisscrossed the small streams along the way, and doubled back several times, making sure they weren't followed. They arrived within sight of the cabin well after dark, but it was a clear night and the moon and stars were out in full, giving off ample light. They rode right up to the small front porch.

Hunter dismounted. Removing his revolver and pulling the hammer back with his thumb, he slowly pushed open the front door. The room was lit up fairly well from the moonlight shining through the crossfire slits carved in the wooden shutters. He looked around, checking the shadowed corners. Certain there were no intruders in the one room cabin, he walked over to the eating table, holstering his Colt as he went. He struck a match, lit a candle, and quickly went back outside.

Hunter looked about the semi-dark terrain while listening for any sign of movement. Satisfied there was no one about, he walked to Lilith where she remained in the saddle on top of her black stallion.

"The coast is clear, my lady," Hunter said, reaching for her as she dismounted. They stood face to face for a moment, then they kissed. Her tongue was soft and alluring, and her smell was maddening. He pushed her away slightly and gently with a small moan, feeling himself becoming aroused. Hunter cleared his throat involuntarily.

"There's water in the basin, if you'd like to go inside and wash up. I need to take care of the horses and put them away for the night." He started to walk away.

But she pulled him back, not letting go of his hands. She stared into his eyes.

"What?" he questioned.

"Be careful," she said.

"It's fine," he said. "There's no one about."

With this assurance, she released him, turned, and walked inside.

Hunter walked the horses through the corral and into the barn. After removing the gear and brushing them down, at a record pace, and measuring out their feed, he washed off in the horse trough. He wished he had time to take a proper bath, but this was not going to happen. Besides, he'd bathed in the river three or four days ago, and it wasn't even summer. He dried off with his bandana, and walked across the front yard and stopping at the cabin door. He rubbed his finger across his front teeth before entering.

The first thing he noticed was the man pants she had been wearing under her dress. They were now hanging over the back of one of the chairs. This excited him. He looked to his left to find her lying in his bed propped up on one elbow, her hair was down, and the covers were barely covering her breasts.

"Make love to me, sir, I beg of you," she pleaded quietly.

Hearing her plea, Hunter kicked the door closed with his boot, then grabbed the three by six plank leaning against the wall, and shoved it in the slots to bar the only entrance to the cabin.

She watched with amusement as he feverishly unbuckled his gunbelt and fumbled around trying to remove his shirt, his boots, his pants, and finally his long johns. She thought he looked magnificent, already standing at attention, with his muscular physique, lightly tanned skin, and many battle scars.

He grabbed his belt that holstered the Colts off the floor and hung them over the bedpost, before crawling under the covers into her waiting arms. They kissed, limbs intertwining while their hands explored each other's bodies. He entered her slowly and deep, as they moaned with pleasure. Her warm juices flowed with excitement. He exploded in her with a passion like she had never felt before. They lay there, breathing heavily, together as one.

They made love several more times that night, each time longer and more passionate than the last. Without words, exhausted, they both fell asleep.

♦❖♦

They surrounded the cabin an hour before dawn. Montgomery and five of his men crept up quietly to the windows and stuck rifles through the bottom of the cross-slits in the shutters, aiming at Hunter and Lilith, who were holding each other, fast asleep.

Richard Montgomery gave the order to fire. The *crack* of the rifles rang out.

Hunter jumped out of bed with a yell, grabbing his revolvers, one in each hand. He stood there naked, glistening with sweat, chest heaving in and out, his head going left then looking right. He looked down to see blood seeping out of several bullet holes in his stomach – they were dead, if this weren't a bad dream.

Now awake, standing there, the blood and bullet holes were gone; they were just a product of his nightmare. He looked down at Lilith. She was on the bed, jammed up against the wall, the covers held up to her neck, eyes wide open.

"What is it?" she demanded.

Hunter lowered his weapons and took a deep breath. "It was a dream, but my dreams are my instincts showed to me in pictures. They are comin' after us; the question is when." Hunter grabbed his drawers off the floor. "If we're going to be together were going to have to ride on and leave this place."

Lilith climbed out of bed and walked over to him, putting her hands on his shoulders.

Hunter followed her with his eyes and his heart. Running from a fight had never, ever, entered his mind anytime in his whole life. But he truly loved this woman, and would do anything to protect her. She was so beautiful, standing there naked before him.

"Hunter James, I will do whatever you say, and go wherever you go, but Richard Montgomery will follow us to the ends of the earth. He is a powerful and vindictive man."

"What are you saying, Lilith?"

"I'm saying, you're going to have to kill him, or we will never have any peace."

"You want me to kill your father?"

"Please sit, my love. We have to talk."

Hunter put his butt on the cold wooden chair and listened to Lilith tell her story. The story of her kidnapping and the murder of her real father, a man named John Bailer.

◆❖◆

Many years back, Richard Montgomery killed Mr. Bailer; he pulled the trigger himself for refusing to sell out his gold claim. Lilith and her father had lived in a small miner's cabin on a claim legally bought in Sacramento. After the death of her mother to smallpox, John sold their farm, and bought the land to pan for gold. The land was covered with mountains, and fresh water springs, and Richard Montgomery would not be satisfied until he owned it all. The tin pans that would not sell were run off or murdered, and her father was the last of the hold outs. This led to his demise.

After the smoke cleared, there stood a dirty-faced, beautiful, thirteen-year-old girl with whom Montgomery immediately fell in love. He took Lilith to be his own. She did not elaborate further. The rest was obvious.

Hunter's expression never changed, but inside, his anger grew.

"Well, it's settled then," Hunter said as he began dressing. "I'm gonna' kill this man, and as many of his men as I have to."

Lilith had begun to dress as well, not knowing where they were going or what they were doing, but instinctively knowing this half-breed gunslinger would protect her to the death.

Hunter and Lilith saddled their horses and emptied the cabin of its food and supplies, loading the pack-horse before heading south toward town. They needed to warn Matt of the situation for the town of Myakka was about to get bloody; and there was the safety of the boy to consider. Zeke and Matt were the only ones in that place Hunter cared about. As far as he was concerned, all the rest could go to hell. He did hope, however, that the doc and his family's home was far enough on the outskirts of Myakka City to keep them safe and away from the line of fire.

They avoided the main roads, traveling on back-woods trails and through untraveled, swampy marshes 'til they arrived behind Matt's Saloon. Hunter dismounted, slid out a Colt, and cocked the hammer back, holding the gun straight up by his head. He slowly opened the back door to the saloon, peering in. With the creak of the door, Matt turned and saw Hunter. He immediately grabbed the trash pail and darted out the back, quickly easing the gunslinger outside closing the door behind them.

"What the hell you doin' here, son? There's three of Montgomery's men in there right now lookin' for ya, and the little lady here. They're the ones Montgomery left behind to watch her, and they ain't none too happy you two went missin'."

"Only three?" replied Hunter.

"They're the only ones in there; everyone else slowly trickled out when they showed. These men are paid killers, Hunter, I have no doubt."

"Matt, I need a place close by where I can hide Lilith."

"Don't I have a say in this?" Lilith demanded, putting her hand on the stock of her Spencer rifle. "This isn't just for looks, I can shoot."

Matt and Hunter looked from her, then to each other. Matt spoke, "We need to git the horses in the barn and you two can hole up in Zeke's loft upstairs. From them upper doors, you can see down the street and the front of the saloon; A good advantage for anyone with a rifle."

"Where's the boy stay, Matt?"

"He done stayed in the barn ever since he showed up in town a few years back. He was dirt from head to toe, eatin' throw outs. He ain't a charity case though, he works for it."

"What happened to his parents?" asked Lilith.

Matt shrugged his shoulders. "Don't rightly know. I ain't never asked, and he ain't never told."

"Is he there now?" asked Hunter.

"He should be up in the loft. I sent him there when those three shooters showed up."

"Good," said Hunter. "We'll hide the horses in the barn and I'll get Lilith and the boy hunkered down in the upstairs. Matt, you go in like nothin's goin' on. Keep their glasses full of that watered down rotgut you call whiskey, until I get there. An' lock that back door behind ya."

"Right," Matt said with a furrowed brow. He mumbled to himself all the way to the door, "My whiskey is some a' the least watered down in these here parts, no need for insults at a time like this."

Hunter and Lilith led the horses from the back of the saloon and into the barn, closing themselves in behind the big, hinged doors. Hunter had begun the checking of his weapons when Zeke came running down the stairs right into Lilith's arms with a big hug.

"Hello, my little man."

"Oh, Miss Lily, it's good to see you! I was so worried!"

Hunter paused, then put his guns away, satisfied they were ready to do their work.

"You two know each other?" he asked, looking mostly toward the boy.

Lilith spoke up, "I've been secretly trying to take care of this boy since the first time I came to these parts two summers ago. I wished to take him back north with me, but father... Richard, said he wouldn't have someone else's bastard living under his roof."

Hunter looked from Lilith to Zeke, his little arms still clutching her waist.

"So what was all that business 'bout 'let me see what I can find out, sir', when you knew all about her, huh, boy?" Hunter asked, clearly irritated.

Zeke hugged Lilith a little tighter, speaking in a low voice, "Well, I figured there would be more coins in it for me if I fed you information a little at a time.

Hunter took a step towards them. "Why you little..!"

"Okay, you two," Lilith broke in, "don't we have more important things to deal with right now?"

"You're right," said Hunter, while sneering a little at the boy, "I'll deal with you later. Right now, I want you two to go up into that loft, with the rifle. Keep an eye down the road for anyone comin'. Shoot to kill, cause they'll be doin' the same, got it?"

Lilith gently broke free from the boy's grasp and walked over to Hunter, giving him a tight hug before whispering in his ear, "You be careful, Mr. James Dolin. Don't make me a widow before I've wed." She turned, grabbed the boy by the hand, and pulled her rifle off her horse. They quickly headed up the stairs to the loft.

Hunter stood there for a moment, thinking, *Did she say wed? What the hell!* He quickly put this out of his mind, heading anxiety off at the pass. For it was time to do what he did best, and he had a plan that put a smile on his face as he slipped out of the barn and disappeared into the woods.

◆❖◆

The three gunmen were still in the saloon. They were drinking and discussing the fact that the half-breed coward wasn't going to show up around here, and was probably halfway to North Carolina by now. Matt kept the whiskey flowing, saying little, and just waiting for the 'you-know-what' to hit the barn door. Up in the loft, Lilith and Zeke were waiting patiently, watching the streets of Myakka.

"Where is he, Lily?" asked Zeke. "He's been gone a while."

"I don't have the slightest, little man. I imagine Matt's wondering the same thing. He better... Wait, what's that at the edge of the woods?"

Hunter came out of the brush at a fast walk, crossing the road and heading straight for the front steps of the Saloon, holding a rattlesnake in each hand.

Zeke spotted the snakes from the loft and gasped, "Holy *shit*! Those are diamond backs, five-footers."

Lilith looked at the boy, ready to reprimand him for bad language, and then she decided against it. What did it matter in this time and place?

She quickly looked back to the street just in time to see her man with two rattlesnakes in a chokehold, a head protruding out the top of each of his clenched fists. They were clearly agitated and squirming around. With one underhand motion, he slung the diamond backs forward. They hit the sandy wood porch and slid under the saloon doors, disappearing out of sight into Matt's place. Hunter took a few steps back, stood at the ready with each hand on the butt of his guns, and waited.

There were sounds of screams, breaking furniture, broken glass, and gunfire coming from inside the saloon. One of the gunmen came out through the swinging doors, pistol in one hand, and holding his snake-bit shin with the other. He stopped at the top of the steps and just stared into Hunter's eyes with a look of anger and questioning confusion.

"Go for it, you're gonna die anyway," announced the gunslinger. "I can see that leg swellin' from here."

With an angry growl, the man raised his gun to fire. Hunter pulled his .44 and put two holes in the man's chest, sending the slower man's bullet into the ground, six inches from Hunter's boot. The snake-bit cowboy fell face first into the dusty street, dead. The half-breed gunslinger spun his gun into the holster with lightning speed, and got back into his stance, resting the palms of his hands on each butt of his Colts.

"You son-of-a-bitch," came a voice from inside. "I'm gonna' kill you!"

A moment later, the doors swung open and the other two men came out firing. Hunter pulled his right-handed colt, with his left palm slamming on the hammer in a downward motion. He emptied the four slugs remaining in the six-shooter, every bullet hitting home, two bullets for one man, two bullets for the other, a done deal.

Hunter methodically, in a cloud of smoke, reloaded his gun while the dead men spewed pools of blood onto the front porch of the saloon.

Matt walked out through the swinging doors with his shotgun in hand. He nudged one of the bodies with his boot, checking for dead.

Hunter was still in his stance, taking the time to look down the street and behind him. He glanced up at the old bartender, feeling it was safe to let down his guard.

"Nice to see you made it. A little late, ain't ya?" announced the gunslinger.

"Hell, son... I been pumpin' thcm thcrc boys with whiskey all mornin'. That ten year old lad in the barn there could a took um out with a slingshot, drunk as they was," the old man replied as he nudged the other body, also checking for dead.

Hunter smiled a little at Matt's banter, and then spoke with matter of fact, "How much time we got?"

"According to Mr. Snake-bit over there, they should be here tomorrow, noon or later."

"That gives us some time; how many?" asked Hunter.

"What I gathered from um, six, maybe ten – don't know fer sure."

"We gotta' get rid of them bodies, Matt. It's warmer today; don't want them to start rottin'."

"I'll fetch Jimmy and the wagon and have him take them to the doc's place at the edge of town. He's got a morgue in the back out there. And if he don't want um, there's plenty of swampy gator pits here'bouts. You,

Lilith, and Zeke need to get up in that loft and come up with some kinda' plan, 'cause I ain't heard one – and get some rest. I'll bring you some food and whiskey in a bit."

Hunter smiled at his old friend, "Thanks for your help, Matt, and you watch yourself, if they think you're helpin' us…"

Matt nodded his head. "I got you, son, but don't you go worryin' 'bout me. You just worry 'bout your woman and that there youngun. Now git."

Hunter entered the barn, taking the stairs to the loft two at a time 'til he reached the top. He was greeted with hugs from both Lilith and Zeke. Lilith had tears of relief in her eyes while the boy went on about how Hunter was the fastest draw in the south, or anywhere in the west for that matter, and when he grew up he would be just as fast.

Hunter could not stop the small grin from growing on his face. He'd never had a family. He'd never loved anyone before. This was a good feeling for him, but it scared him nonetheless. He had always been able to take care of himself, but now he had others to worry about. The gunslinger had been a loner all his life, now that seemed to have changed overnight.

Hunter's father had been long gone before he was born which left the tribe to raise him but never as one of them. He was treated like the bastard that he was. He was constantly teased and forced to defend himself from the older Indian boys. One night after a severe beating, he stole a bow, arrows, and a hunting knife, along with food and water. He went deep into the swamps moving north, thinking of his father. Maybe the white man would be more accepting of him, he did not know. Hunter was in his tenth year, free at last and on his own. That seemed so long ago. He never did find his father, and soon gave up searching, but he did become a man, and learned the white man's ways, mastering the white man's gun. Hunter's tracking skills were self-taught and forced upon him early. It is amazing how quickly you learn to track animals when you are starving.

In his early teens, he ran across a small band of Union soldiers lost in the swamps. They were five men, hungry, and scarred up, their necks and face's red and puffy with mosquito bites. The young half-breed saved their lives. He made natural medicine from marsh plants to heal their insect wounds, avoiding infection. He killed a three hundred pound hog with two arrows through its side, ending its life by slitting the animal's throat with his bowie knife. The young half -breed's cooking skills were about as good as his hunting skills, and the soldiers became indebted to him.

Hunter led them out of the Florida swamps, north into Georgia, delivering them safely into the hands of their regiment. Hunter was rewarded with guns and a job – tracking down Indians for the United States Army. They taught him to shoot, drink, and gamble. Everything a man needed to know. Even though he was a man among many men, he was still part Injun, a loner – and considered by many, the enemy.

He now stood with his arms around a beautiful woman and a fine boy, thinking he'd finally found what he'd been searching for his whole life. A family, he swore to himself, he would not let anything or anyone, ever come between them.

◆❖◆

Jimmy had fetched the wagon and brought it around to the front of the saloon, where Matt helped him load the three bodies.

"Jimmy, run these bodies up to the doc's place. Tell him and anyone else you come across to hunker down or leave town."

"How bad is it gonna' be, boss?" Jimmy asked. He continued without letting Matt answer, "You know I don't git in no one's affairs, I just do what you tell me."

"I'm tellin' ya', after the doc's, you take the wagon and the horses and git on out of town to your sister's place, and stay there. Bessie's already there, I sent her this mornin'."

"Fer how long?" Jimmy asked.

Matt was getting a little irritated. He knew Jimmy didn't get along with his sister, that's why he was working and living here, at the saloon. For a man that didn't get in anyone's business, he always asked a lot of questions.

"Damnit, Jimmy, don't argue with me! Just git goin'."

"I ain't arguin' with yaws, boss, I's just askin', gees." Jimmy snapped the reins, moving the horses and the wagon down the road.

Matt could hear him complaining and mumbling 'til he was out of, what Matt liked to call, bitchin' distance.

Matt looked up and down the street. There was no one around. The few shops in town were locked up tight. The word had gotten out that big trouble was coming. As far as he could tell, everyone had skedaddled. The old man entered his saloon, setting the shotgun on the bar with the barrels facing the front door. He grabbed up both dead rattlesnakes, walked around behind the bar, and laid them up on top of the counter. He pulled two bottles of whiskey from underneath, opening one and taking a long welcome swig.

After a deep breath, Matt said aloud, "I'm gitin' way too old for this shit,"

Hunter walked in.

Matt quickly put his hand on the shotgun's stock, his finger on the trigger. After seeing who it was, his hand went from the gun to his face, rubbing his chin whiskers.

"A little jumpy there, ain't ya', old man," Hunter commented as he bellied up to the bar.

With a glare, Matt handed him the open bottle.

The half-breed took a long draw. Hunter looked at the diamondbacks, pointing with his thumb, "Dinner?"

"Waste not, want not." replied Matt.

"You know how to clean and cook that kind a' varmint?" Hunter asked, knowing damn well the old timer did. He was just trying to ease the predicament they had found themselves in.

"I was skinnin' and cookin' rattlers before you were a scratch in your daddy's britches."

"Can't you ever just answer yes or no?" asked Hunter.

"I found in all my years that yes and no answers don't add much to a conversation." Matt said with a grin, before opening the other bottle for himself.

Hunter turned back to the serious matter at hand. "Matt, you're too old for this. It's my fight, so why don't you git out a' town for a few days and I'll take care of this mess."

Matt pulled two cigars out of his top pocket and handed one to Hunter. They both bit the ends off, spitting them on the floor and lighting up.

"You're right, son. I might be too old for this, but I'll tell you somethin'... I was born here, I was the first one to build here, and I'm goin' to die here. No rich Yankee is gonna' run me off without a fight. Besides, we can hang together or we will for sure hang separately, so do we have a plan yet or what?"

"Didn't someone important say that?"

"Yeah, me, now what's the plan?"

"Right now, the only plan I got is to kill everybody without gittin' shot, but I'll think of somethin'."

They clanked whiskey bottles and drank to their backwoods profoundness.

CHAPTER SEVEN

Early the next morning just after the sun had come up, Montgomery and his men were headed back to Myakka. Richard had gotten the word his Lilith was running with the half-breed. She was trying to escape him, which wasn't a surprise. She had tried before, but with that savage, *that* was unacceptable. They both must die. He didn't care who took the gunslinger out, but he wanted to kill Lilith himself. She made a fool out of him. His reputation was at stake and he couldn't let something like this stand. It was possible the men he left behind may have already killed them, but he couldn't count on it. Those three were far from his best, and they were more than likely no match for Hunter James Dolin.

Montgomery found himself with only six men, after three cowardly souls snuck out of his camp in the middle of the night. They knew who they would be facing, and wanted no part of it. This forced Richard to go where he sat now, across the kitchen table from Frank Lugar at the Big L Ranch.

"What can I do for you, Montgomery?" asked Frank.

"Please, call me Richard, We're amongst friends here," he said, his gaze moving about the room.

"All right then, Richard, call me Frank. But let's cut the bullshit. We've never been friends. We've decided that these lands were big enough for the both of us, so why don't you just tell me what you want."

"Okay, Frank, if that's how you want it, I'll cut to the chase. You and I have a mutual problem. His name is Hunter James Dolin."

Frank's expression did not change. His poker face was working particularly well this morning. Frank signaled to the Chinaman, who set a glass in front of Montgomery and filled it with whiskey.

Richard picked up the glass, but did not drink until the chink filled Frank's glass and Frank drank first. Chinn Yang filled both their glasses once again, set the bottle on the table, and left the room.

"I've got to git me one of those." said Montgomery, pointing toward the door Chinn Yang had gone through.

"Best money I ever spent," replied Frank.

"Now, back to the matter at hand. Yeah, I heard Dolin killed three of your men yesterday, and he might be fornicating with your daughter, or *whoever* she is. How does any of that make it my problem?"

The look on Richard's face made every man in the room tense up, their hands sliding instinctively to the butts of their guns.

"Easy, boys," said Richard. "I'm gonna' let that remark go, because I know this half-breed savage son-of-a-bastard is a problem for you too. Everybody knows you killed his father, shot in the back, as I recall, and that won't be forgotten."

Now it was Frank's turn to project the evil eye. "There's no proof of that."

"You know as well as I do, you don't need proof in these parts," explained Richard. "Rumors will do. Now, are we gonna' work together or not?"

"All right then," agreed Frank. "But we need some leverage. This one's clever."

Frank told Richard he believed Hunter ambushed four of his men back on a trail they knew well. He also told of a rumor he heard recently of two six-foot rattlesnakes that were thrown into Matt's saloon, just before three fleeing men were gunned down in the street.

Richard Montgomery wasn't scared easily, but even he was concerned. *Frank's right,* thought Richard. *We need some leverage.* And he knew just what that leverage should be.

CHAPTER EIGHT

After a breakfast of cold rattlesnake and jerky with Lilith and the boy, Hunter decided he had to get them out of town. They were too close to the action. It would be risky, but it was the only way. If he was worrying about protecting them, it could cloud his judgment and put him at a definite disadvantage in a gunfight where they were already greatly outnumbered.

After some arguing and bickering, and pleas for all of them to leave this place together, Lilith finally agreed to take the boy to Hunter's cabin. By now, Hunter figured Montgomery and his men knew they were holed up in town. The plan was for Lilith and Zeke to go in a back way to the cabin, which the boy knew. They would stash the horses in the thicket at the river, and cross on foot at a shallow area. After wiping away their tracks with palm fronds, they would stay in the barn, under the hay if necessary. Lilith had her rifle, and Matt gave the boy an old, but working, revolver.

"Do you know how to use this, son?" asked Hunter.

"Yes sir, Matt learned me when I was eight. I shot a squirrel right in the head! I'll shoot anyone I got to!" Zeke exclaimed proudly, all bowed up like a game rooster.

Hunter smiled and patted the boy on the back. "You're a brave little man, Zeke. And when this is all over, we'll spend some time together and I'll teach you lots of things, okay?"

"Yes sir, that would be better than a stick whoopin'!"

Hunter rubbed the boy's head, messing up his hair, and then turned his attention to Lilith. Reaching out, he brought her into his arms, kissing her passionately. Hunter shortened the kiss, feeling Zeke's eyes upon them.

"Be careful," Hunter pleaded. "And do like we planned. There's enough food and water on the packhorse for at least five days. If you don't hear from me in two, head north to Fort Meade. You might get some help there."

Lilith began to tear up as she mounted her stallion. Hunter made a cup with his hands; Zeke put his left foot in them and was slung up onto the back of the saddle.

"I'll be there to fetch ya' tomorrow or the next day, I promise." Hunter said with a wink. Then he smacked the horse on the hindquarters, sending it into a gallop. With the packhorse in tow, he watched them as they rode off out of town.

◆❖◆

Shortly past sunup, and if the information that Matt got from the now dead rattlesnake boys was true, Montgomery and his men were due anytime. With Lilith and the boy headed for safety, and the town deserted, Hunter and Matt still needed to prepare for their guests to arrive. They were in the saloon quietly having their beer and stogies, when Matt broke the silence.

"If your plan is for killin', Hunter James, I got somethin' to show ya' that might be of some help." He waved his hand, motioning for Hunter to follow him. "Foller me."

Matt took the gunslinger upstairs to his room, where he opened the door and stepped aside for Hunter to enter. Looking around, he saw a single-framed bed next to a small table with an empty washbasin on top. The only thing that wasn't ordinary was in the corner of the room. It appeared to be a two-foot long by two-foot high by two-foot wide iron box. Hunter walked over, and knelt down in front of it. He looked back to Matt who was still standing in the doorway.

Matt nodded. "Open it up. Go easy, though. It's old and might be a tad unstable."

Hunter opened the lid, and easily dug through the hay with his hand.

"The hay keeps it dry, don't want it sweatin'," explained Matt.

"Dynamite!" Hunter said with a grin. "Old man, you're full a' surprises. This could definitely give us an edge."

"I got one plunger, and so many feet of powder cord for a big boom. The other sticks will have to be lit by their fuse, or gunfire."

"This is good, Matt," said Hunter. "Let's get busy."

There was a handle on each side of the box, Hunter grabbed one end, and Matt grabbed the other. They began carefully walking the paper-wrapped sticks of blasting powder down the stairs.

"Where we headed?" Matt grunted, feeling a tightness to his lower back.

"To the Jackson Hotel, if your old bones can make it across the street."

"Do we have a plan now, you reckon?" Matt asked, deciding to ignore Hunter's sarcastic banter.

"You can call it that, if it makes you feel better. I figure, with them out-numberin' us they might get careless, and if I can get them to come after me, we can even up the odds just a bit."

Hunter rigged up Montgomery's hotel with the dynamite, in case they got into trouble and had to retreat. Matt would be staked out up in the loft behind bales of hay that were now stacked across the upper doors. With this higher view, he could see down the street, limiting the surprise in the gunman's attack. By planting a rifle at each end of the open doors, Matt could slide back and forth, reload, and move back again, covering more area at different angles. Hunter would be camped out just inside the saloon, firing from the side at ground level. Both men had as much extra ammo as they could carry, which they borrowed from the deserted gun shop. Hunter had his Colts and his shotgun. Matt had his Henry rifle, and Hunter's rifle. Plus, for the first time in ages – barely fitting around his waist – hung Matt's six shooters.

Hunter also set up what he liked to call a 'bang' swing. This was sticks of powder tied to the low hanging branch of a tree, which he set up to swing out and over across from the saloon and in front of the barn reaching the center of the road. With this done, all there was to do now was wait, eat jerky, and sip some whiskey.

◆ ❖ ◆

Little did they know, thirty minutes south someone picked up Lilith and the boy's trail and was following them.

He'd been sent out that morning to scout out the situation in town, and to locate Lilith and the half-breed. The extremely large, part Cajun, part Injun, swamp-raised cracker named Gator was an excellent tracker, and knew these areas better than anyone. Gator worked his way up the river, heading south toward town. He figured this route would be the most likely if they tried to sneak out of Myakka and attempt an escape to the north. He found not a sign, other than some deer tracks, so he doubled back and crossed the stream to the other side of the bank.

Gator knew the half-breed wouldn't run; he would stay and fight. It was bred into him. That's why he was surprised to find the horse tracks. Someone took the back way to the gunslinger's cabin, two sets of horse tracks. It now made some sense to Gator, to hide her here. The white bosses wouldn't expect it. They would figure he would keep her close to him in town, where he could protect her.

Gator dismounted and got down on one knee for a closer inspection. There was an attempt to cover the tracks, and he immediately knew this was not the work of the gunslinger. He followed their trail, which led him away from the creek toward the woods. Walking his horse with him, he found a small clearing. There, tied to a tree, was a black stallion and a loaded packhorse. The Cajun left his Chickasaw pony and made his way back to the water. He crossed at the same shallow area of the creek, where the covered tracks ended.

Rifle in hand, and stalking with cat-like movements, he made his way across the field to the back of the cabin. Working his way around to the front, he poised to kick in the door when he heard a slight sound coming from the barn. The Gator Man's head snapped around. He stood there motionless, listening intently. There it was again. He left the front of the cabin and went toward the barn.

He worked his way to a small window, peering in. There, lying on the hay was the woman and a young boy he recognized from the stables, sound asleep. With the striking speed of a snake, Gator kicked open the barn door. Three strides of his long legs had him standing in front of the boy and the woman.

The crash of the door sent Lilith and Zeke jerking up into a sitting position. For a split second, they saw a towering shadow of a man, before their lights went out with a one, two rifle butt to the face.

They were both bruised and bloody, knocked out cold. Lilith's right upper cheek was swelling up, and the boy's forehead was knotting. This meant nothing to the Gator Man. He tied their hands together and then their feet with twine he found in the barn. With one arm around each body, he slung them up and over his shoulders, grabbing his rifle, and moving on out the door. For most men, the long walk through the field and the crossing of the creek with this weight would be nearly an impossible feat, but not for this man. Years ago, his living consisted of dragging much heavier gators this same way, at further distances through treacherous swamps.

He made his way to the horses, draping the lifeless bodies over the black stallion, tying them off for travel. He left the packhorse behind to fend for itself.

Gator talked aloud to no one in particular, as he mounted his horse and headed back the way he'd come. "This job ain't very challengin', but it sure pays better than sellin' gator meat and rattlesnake hides. Yep, the white bosses will be pleased when they see what I done brought um."

◆❖◆

Hunter and Matt sat at their posts all afternoon, looking for the trouble that did not come. Hunter was stationed in the saloon, and the old man was up in the loft of the barn. It was dark now and Hunter cat-napped on and off, always aware of his surroundings. Matt, on the other hand, could be heard snoring from time to time all the way down the deserted street.

Well, Hunter thought, *this is one hell of an army I got here.*

Did they stand a chance, he wondered? Probably not, but hell, they didn't have nothing better to do. This wasn't true either. He could take Lilith and the boy and leave this place to start anew, but the nature of his pride seemed to be more important. The only thing Hunter could figure was Montgomery was waiting them out, trying to catch them with little or no rest; evidently, they didn't know Matt's sleeping habits very well.

Would they attack at night? Hunter didn't think so. Their best advantage would be to come early morning, at first light. Being convinced of this, Hunter poured a bucket of beer, and grabbed a glass jar of jerky from behind the bar before exiting out the back. He walked around the saloon, down the alleyway and across the street to the front door of the barn. At the foot of the stairs, he started to yell up to his old friend, to let him know who it was, when he heard snoring. He quietly went up, planning to give Matt a start.

But when he got to the top and poked his head around the corner rail, there was Matt, sitting in a chair pointing his pistol right at Hunter – still making the snoring sound, with his eyes open.

"Maybe if you were all Injun instead of half, I wouldn't a' heard ya' comin' up them stairs."

"I'm impressed, old man, but you're always breaking my balls."

"That's just my way," Matt replied proudly. "So what do you think, son? Why ain't them boys showed yet?"

"I don't rightly know. With their numbers, I didn't reckin' they would be cautious. I thought they would ride in here like wolves after a deer."

Hunter set down the jerky and handed the bucket of beer over to Matt, after taking a sip of his own. "Here you go, old timer. I brought you some foamy pick-me-up."

"Well, thank ya'. Maybe you're not the savage everyone says you are." Matt commented as he buried his face into the bucket, tipping it back, taking a long draw of the brew.

Not in the mood for a back and forth, Hunter walked over behind the bales of hay and stood at the open loft doors. He stared down the dark road and lit a smoke.

"I just can't figure where Montgomery and his men are holed up at. Hell, maybe they were delayed gittin' back. With any luck they were scalped by Indians and are layin' dead in the swamp somewheres."

Matt let out a loud belch as he left his chair and walked over to Hunter's side, gazing out into the night.

"Now, you know, Mr. James Dolin, men like us don't have that kind of luck."

"Shush, you hear that?" Hunter said, holding up his hand to stop Matt from talking.

"I don't hear nothin', said Matt. "No wait..." He could hear it then, a horse and wagon coming up the road toward them, fast. Hunter and Matt simultaneously cocked their rifles and aimed them in the direction of the charging wagon. The rig rolled up and stopped in front of the barn. The driver was unaware of the two rifles up above aimed at his head.

"Doc!" Matt hollered. What the hell're you doin' down there?"

"Matt, Hunter, thank God I found you! I got news. Montgomery and his men have partnered up with Frank Luger out at his ranch."

"Where'd you hear this?" asked Hunter.

"Earlier today..." The doc was trying to catch his breath. "A couple of Frank's men came to see me for some doctorin', one of them had cut his hand on some fence wire. They were goin' on about how they should have no trouble takin' you two out, now that Frank and Montgomery had teamed up and all."

"They talked of this right in front of ya'? Were they foolin'?" Matt asked the doctor.

"It weren't no set up, if that's what you mean. These boys weren't too smart. They didn't think I'd do anythin' to warn ya'."

"All right, Doc," said Hunter, "you git back home and hunker down. Come mornin' you're gonna' git some business, and hopefully it ain't us."

"Good luck," said Doc, as he slapped the reins and steered the wagon back the way he'd come, leaving the two men, and the empty town behind.

◆❖◆

Morning seemed to creep up quickly on Hunter and Matt, but they were rested, fed, and prepared – as well as they could be for what was coming. Hunter didn't know if their foes would all come at once, or if they would attack in waves. He was hoping for the latter.

The blasting powder sticks might even up the odds somewhat, but for the most part it was going to be bullet for bullet, may the best shooters win. That's when Hunter decided to stay upstairs in the loft with Matt, where he could get a better lowdown on the incoming gun men.

What was it Matt had said? Hunter thought. *Hang together, or we'll surely hang alone.*

The sun was peeking over the buildings when the first wave hit. Two wagons came thundering up the road, one in front of the other, a single horse per wagon with one rider on each. The riders rode on the horses, leaving the wagon seats empty.

Hunter and Matt had their rifles aimed at the drivers, waiting to see what they would do next. The men and their wagons turned, stopping nose to tail in line with the barn, a hundred feet away. They either knew or had guessed that Hunter and Matt were in the loft.

The riders cut the leather traces connected to the horses and rode on, leaving the wagons behind. They turned their animals back the way they had come for their escape. They didn't make it. Both cowboys jerked and then fell off their horses after one bullet from Hunter's rifle and another from Matt's.

As the crackers fell dead to the ground, ten more men rode in. Jumping down from their saddles, they tipped the wagons on their sides to form a wall.

Before they completed this task, Hunter killed two and Matt slightly wounded another.

Gaining their positions behind the wagons, a mixture of Luger men and Montgomery men opened fire on the barn. Splinters of shattering wood flew in all directions. The bales of hay vibrated violently from the constant flow of bullets hitting them.

After diving for cover, Hunter knew it was time for the 'bang' swing. While there was a lull in the action for reloading, Hunter lay across a bale of hay in the far corner of the open doors and aimed his rifle barrel at the line of eucalyptus trees to the side of the road. So far, luck was running in his favor. The bad guys had positioned themselves in the road, almost directly across from the tree that held the trap.

The bang swing had five pieces of the powder sticks tied to one end of a long rope; the other end was tied to a high branch of an overhanging tree. There was a two-pound rock tied to this rope, three feet above the sticks. There was a smaller line tied to the same rope between the rock and the powder; the other end of the small line was pulled back in the woods and tied to another tree. Shoot the small line and it would release the rope, allowing it to swing out over the road, approximately ten feet above the ground. Then shoot the dynamite.

Hunter could hear Matt firing to his right as bullets whizzed by his head, coming from the men out front. Hunter aimed, and then fired at the small line. The bullet hit its target, breaking the line, and releasing the 'bang' swing. Holding his breath, Hunter followed the bundle of blasting powder sticks with the sight of his rifle as it swung out over the wagons and the shooting men. He pulled the trigger.

Ka-boom! Wagon wood went up and out like shrapnel; the men were thrown and scattered, body parts flew along with sand and black smoke. When the flying kindling and smoke cleared, there was no one left alive.

Standing up from behind the bales of hay, Hunter yelled down from the loft, "Yeah..! Did ya' see that, Matt? Worked just like it was s'pose to." Looking over to his right, Hunter saw that the front porch of the saloon was also destroyed by the concussion of the blast. Luckily, it had not caught fire.

"Sorry 'bout the saloon, Matt."

"No matter," said the old timer. "Way to go, son... Looked like the fourth of Jew-lie."

Hunter immediately noticed the weak sound of the old man's voice. He walked over to the stairs where Matt was sitting on the floor, his back against the wall. His revolver held in his left hand, his right hand was holding his belly as blood seeped between his fingers. Hunter knelt on one knee.

"How bad is it, Matt? You want I should fetch Doc?"

"Don't bother with it, son." Matt coughed. "They got me. I'm gut shot."

"I'm sorry, Matt." Sorrow filled Hunter's voice as he bowed his head, staring to the floor.

At that moment, from behind Hunter's right side, he heard a slight creak on the floor boards.

Matt yelled, "Look out!" and fired his revolver. He shot Jake Lugar, who had appeared behind Hunter at the top of the stairs. Little Johnny was coming up right behind his brother Jake. Johnny fired, hitting Matt, just before Hunter put two bullets in his head.

Hunter heard the bodies falling down the steps, but something, or someone, seemed to slow their journey to the bottom. He holstered his pistol, pulled out the sawed-off shotgun and went to the top of the stairs. He looked down and there stood Frank Luger at the bottom, gun drawn, staring at his sons' lifeless bodies.

"You killed my boys," said Frank, his voice breaking. He didn't look up from them.

"You killed my pa," replied Hunter.

Frank raised his head, staring into the gunslinger's eyes. "I guess this makes us even, *half-breed.*"

"No," said Hunter, slowly raising the shotgun, "not yet."

Frank dropped his revolver and brought his arms up head high, palms out as if to block something.

Feeling no mercy, the gunslinger pulled both triggers; blood splattered the walls in a thundering boom as both barrels shredded Frank's hands before taking his face. Hunter quickly reloaded the shotgun as he went down the stairs, stepping over the bodies to the first floor. There was no one else, all was quiet. He quickly headed back up the steps to the loft, kneeling next to Matt. There was nothing more to be done, he was dead.

Hunter stood. He reloaded his revolver, followed by his rifle. He picked up Matt's rifle and was loading it when he heard Montgomery's voice coming from the outside and down below.

"Half-bree-e-ed... Come out and see what I got!"

The gunslinger walked over to the open loft doors carrying a rifle in each hand. He looked down onto the road, and though no one would have known by his facial expression, his heart sank at what he saw. Lined up side-by-side on horseback, was Montgomery and six of his men. Next to Montgomery was the big man they called Gator, and in front of him sat Lilith, riding double, looking dirty and beaten. Montgomery had his pistol barrel pushed against the temple of her head.

"All right, Dick!" Hunter yelled down. "Here's the deal. You let her ride out, and I won't kill ya'."

Montgomery laughed an evil laugh. "First of all, half-breed, my name is Richard, and you're in no position to deal. And if you were, I don't make deals." After a pause, he continued, "I've got a better idea, why don't you just say goodbye, right now?"

Montgomery pulled the trigger and the shot rang out.

All Hunter could see was splattering chunks of red hit the horseman next to Lilith, as she fell to the ground.

"*No-o-o-o!*" Hunter screamed. Dropping one rifle, he began firing with the other, but his rage affected his aim and he only killed two. They were not the two he had wanted. The remaining four, including Montgomery and Gator, took cover behind some dead horses and what was left of the wagons.

Hunter dove behind a bale of hay, avoiding the return fire. It seemed to him fairly even, him against four, except for one thing. He was getting low on ammo and these men had just joined this little shindig. He was sure he would run out of bullets before all of them.

Hunter felt distraught and overwhelmed with the unfamiliar emotions of grief and despair. He must push the feelings aside if he wanted to survive. Lilith was dead. The only thing he could do now was to avenge her death, with his last breath if necessary. He would lure them all into Montgomery's Hotel. The problem was he might have to get shot to do it.

The gunslinger grabbed Matt's rifle, stood up, and ran sideways across the loft opening, firing until the gun was empty then dropping it to the ground. Their return fire missed him. He made his way down the stairs to the ground floor, where he stepped out the back door.

Outside now, he put his back to the wall. He was breathing hard and he could feel the adrenaline pumping through his veins. Hunter looked around; there was no one about. He would have to run from the corner of the barn toward them to reach the front door of the Jackson Hotel. As fast as he was, he would most likely catch a bullet; but that was the plan, wasn't it? To be wounded enough where they would come in after him – but not so much where he couldn't make it out the back to the edge of the ravine. Some plan, but it must work – for him to end this. *Matt would be happy,* he thought, *at least he finally had a plan.*

"Vengeance is mine say'th the Lord," he quoted quietly. He had heard someone read this from an old book once. He was a man made in God's image, so he figured he was also entitled to have his revenge.

He took off from the corner of the barn with his revolver in his left hand, firing across his chest to his right. For a moment there was nothing, and then they spotted him and began firing with everything they had.

Bullets whizzed by his head and kicked up dirt by his feet; he dropped his empty gun and jumped full stride, feet first, onto the front porch of the hotel. He couldn't believe it; he'd made it without a scratch. As soon as this thought crossed his mind he felt a bullet go through his side, and then another nicked the back of his upper leg as he dove inside through the door.

Hunter rolled out of the doorway to a window. He pulled his other revolver, and after breaking the glass, fired all six shots in their general direction. As an afterthought, he threw the empty gun out the broken window into the street for all to see.

That sealed the deal. The pain in his leg and torso hurt like hell, but he managed to stand and peer out the corner of the window. He heard and saw what he needed.

"Get him, boys, he's wounded!" Montgomery yelled, "Now get in there an' finish him off!"

They came fast.

Hunter stood up and limped as quickly as he could to the large picture window at the back of the hotel. He pulled out the shotgun from his side holster, shattering the glass with the butt end. He turned and waited, watching the front doors.

All of them busted through at once, eager to get at him.

He dove through the window with a roll to his feet and limped as he ran through the soft sand to the ravine, sliding feet first at the edge, and turning on his belly. He waited to see them looking out the back. They all showed, guns in hand, one, two, three, four – close enough.

Staring at him with the plunger box in his hand, they realized what was happening only a half-second before Hunter pushed down on the tee handle, blowing them all to pieces.

The explosion was enormous. Hunter rolled down the hill to the wet, muddy bottom where he was showered with wood and glass to the point of total darkness. Then, there was nothing.

◆❖◆

He was suddenly awakened by both pressure and pain. The first thought that came to him was he must have been buried alive. Lying on his stomach, his face was cold and wet with mud; and there was heavy warm weight on his back. He couldn't move. He felt he must or he would die, or maybe he was dead already. He was groggy and confused.

His hands were under him, palms down under his chest, so he tried pushing up. There was movement. *What was it?* He could smell burnt pine wood. *It's a piece of wall on my back.*

His memory came flooding back just then, and the explosion of the hotel reverberated in his ears. He now felt the pain where he had been shot in his side and then his leg, but this did not compare to the pain he felt within. Lilith was dead. Matt was dead.

Forever's a long time, is it not? As Lilith might say. For the first time, it suddenly dawned on him, *Where was the boy? Where was Zeke?* Hunter James Dolin would never get the answer to this question if he didn't get out of this damn ditch.

With everything he had in him, he pushed up and up, the weight finally gave way and he quickly rolled to his left out from under the partial wood wall on top of him.

He laid there on his back for a moment smelling smoke. Then, struggling to his feet he lumbered up the slope of the ravine. At the top, he could see most of the town was on fire. He made his way to the edge of the blown-out building that was once the hotel. He looked around on the ground, looking, searching... There it was, the gunslinger picked up his shotgun, checked the shells, and limped to the center of what was left of the city of Myakka.

He slowly made his way over to the barn. Parts of it were blown away and smoldering, but the loft was still intact, so he headed up the stairs. He stopped at the top and looked down at Matt with his back against the wall, sitting in a pool of his own blood.

"I've never seen you so quiet," Hunter said softly, "You always had somethin' to say about somethin'."

Matt did not answer.

"Goodbye, my old friend."

Hunter retrieved his rifle and found the bottle of whiskey they were sharing, before all hell had broken loose. Hunter took a long draw off the bottle and wandered outside. He avoided the middle of the road, knowing Lilith's lifeless body would be there. He just could not bear to look upon her. He avoided gazing in her direction, as he looked around. He was alone. He looked up, staring at the darkening sky.

"What's a man gotta' do to get a horse around here?" he yelled.

Once again, he didn't get an answer.

He downed the rest of the whiskey bottle and threw it at what was left of Matt's Saloon. It bounced off a few pieces of debris, before finally shattering. More thoughts came to him, *Is it likely that horse of mine is still tied up behind the buildin'? After all the gunfire, and then the explosion?* He didn't know, but there was only one way to find out. Around the building he went.

The Appaloosa was no longer tied to the post where he had left him. He looked north, nothing. He looked south and, to Hunter's surprise; there was the App, grazing on a pall meadow bush. Hunter walked up slowly and mounted the steed. They left town at a walk.

"Remind me to give you a name someday, Horse," Hunter said as he rounded the corner to the main road, heading out the same way he'd come just over a season ago. "I think you've earned it."

Hunter passed under the Myakka sign at the end of town, or at the beginning of town, depending on which way you were heading. He stood up on the back of his yet to be named horse, and took out his Bowie knife. He crossed out the six of the number 60, after the word Population, leaving the zero.

With most of the empty town now ablaze, the half-breed gunslinger rode out with only one thing on his mind, find the boy named Zeke, dead or alive.

CHAPTER NINE

Hunter's eyes opened slowly. There was dim light. He stared for a moment trying to focus, *Wood planks?* He tried to think, but his head hurt. *I'm still in the ravine,* he thought, *buried under debris.*

Hunter's eyes opened slowly, again. He must have dozed off. He didn't know for how long. The gunslinger reached up and felt his forehead, rubbing it. He felt the bandage wrapped tightly around it. He struggled to lift up onto his elbows, feeling a wincing pain in his lower chest as he did so. He felt around his mid-section, outlining another tight bandage as he looked around the small room.

The walls were made of limestone and the floor was moist dirt, the musty smell told him he was under-ground. Hunter groaned as he rose fully to a sitting position atop the cot. There to his right were his guns and the rest of his clothes, along with his boots. As his eyes focused in and out, he noticed there was a set of stairs leading to a door in the ceiling. Dressing as quickly as he was able, and arming himself with one of his revolvers, making sure to check it for a full cylinder, he headed up.

With his gun drawn, he slowly pushed up on the door at the top of the steps. The light made his eyes squint and the aroma of fatback hit his sense of smell hard, making his mouth water.

Doc turned around and, leaving the food to cook on its own, he quickly pulled the door in the floor upward, helping Hunter out and sitting him down in a chair at the kitchen table.

"Thank the Lord," said the Doc. "You made it, son. It was touch and go, there for a bit."

Hunter sat there, staring at this man, questioning him with a look that said *where* and *how*?

"Where are you? And how did you get here?" asked Doc, correctly reading the gunslinger's face.

Hunter nodded, wincing slightly at the pain in his head.

"That's a good sign, both good questions. Lucky for you, you have a hard head."

Doc plated up some bacon and set it in front of his battered looking friend, along with a tin cup half-full of coffee.

"You eat, son, and I'll explain it to ya'. You've been out for three days."

"Three days?" grunted Hunter, as he removed the bandage from his head. The gunslinger drank his coffee in one gulp and began to devour the bacon strips from his plate.

"You got anythin' stronger than this?" he asked, as he held up his tin.

The doctor reached up in the cabinet and grabbed a bottle of whiskey, setting it down in front of Hunter.

He pulled the cork and took a swig. "All right, Doc, what the hell happened?"

Doc, an empty tin in his hand, sat down at the kitchen table across from Hunter. He filled it three-quarters to the rim with the golden brew, before he began to explain.

◆❖◆

Doc knew a war was coming. He didn't think that his home was far enough away from the action, so he sent his family north. He was reluctant to do this, for the journey could possibly be more dangerous than staying put. Indians, rustlers and just plain bad men were plentiful in these parts, but when the Doc heard the explosion, followed by seeing smoke billowing up on the horizon, his mind was easily made.

After his family's departure, he waited half a day for anyone who might show up, wounded or not, friend or foe. When no one came, he loaded up the wagon with his medical bag, food, water, and whiskey, before heading toward town. The Doc was a third of the way there, when just off the wagon trail he came across Hunter, slumped in the saddle, passed out cold, while the Appaloosa grazed on patches of wild Bahia grass.

Doc had heaved him into the wagon; he looked him over through the filth and dried blood that covered him. He found two bullet holes, luckily only flesh wounds. When he checked his eyes, Hunter appeared to have a concussion, so with the gunslinger's horse in tow, he brought them back to his home. After cleaning him up and doctoring him, he hid the gunslinger in the room under the kitchen floor.

That was almost three days ago.

◆❖◆

Hunter was listening intently and feeling much better after finishing several cups of coffee. The whiskey helped the pain in his head and the bacon was bringing his strength back.

"Where's Matt, Lilith, and the boy?" asked Doc, while refilling his own cup with whiskey.

"Matt's dead and Zeke's missin'. I was hoping you knew where the boy was."

"I haven't seen hide nor hair of anyone. That's why I was out lookin', when I came across you." There was silence for a time as they drank, staring into their tins.

"Hunter, what happened to Lilith?" asked Doc, once again.

Hunter couldn't speak of it; he just continued searching for something in the bottom of his cup. After a moment, he forced the words out, "Montgomery – he shot her in the head."

"Oh, I'm so, so sorry, son. Did you git that soulless son-of-a-bitch?"

Hunter lifted his head up and looked directly at Doc with piercing steel blue eyes. "I got um. I got them all. The town's burnt to the ground by now."

"You might have killed all the men in town," said Doc, "but there's still some of Frank Lugar's boys holed up out at the ranch. That would be the only place I can think of, where Zeke might be."

With that last statement from Doctor Harmon, Hunter stood and walked over, lifting the trapdoor and disappearing through the floor.

The doctor held it open for him on his return, as his arms were full of his remaining gear. Hunter, now completely dressed, checked the shotgun and the rifle, making sure they were locked and loaded as he had done a thousand times before.

"Doc, I'm goin' up there to that ranch and find the boy. You can sit tight or head north, your choice."

"I might only be a Doctor, but I'm no coward, James Dolin. I can shoot a scattergun like any other."

"I know you can, Doc, but I'm goin' it alone. There's enough dead bodies around here 'cause of me, and I'm not sure my conscience can handle anymore." Hunter stared at the doctor, a glare of rage and regret.

It made the man squirm inside, just a bit.

"So don't argue with me," the gunslinger continued, "or I'll knock you out and stuff you down in that lime-rock jail of yours; got it?"

"I don't like it, son," said the doc, "but I understand. It's settled then, I'm going north to search out my family, and hope they haven't found any trouble."

Doc had taken good care of the Appaloosa. Outside now, Hunter saddled the steed through the pain of his battered ribs, at the same time feeling good about his clearing head. The bullet wounds were healing nicely and showed no sign of infection.

He shook the doctor's hand while thanking him for being there before mounting and riding north towards Lugar's ranch. That was the last time he would ever see the good Doctor.

- 92 -

CHAPTER TEN

Hunter James Dolin was a man who lived with strength and skill, and he would need all of that to survive another battle, especially in his current condition. The sun was approaching three hours past straight up as he moved along. He stayed off the main road, riding through the swampy sawgrasses that lay on the other side of the tree line, avoiding the open roads and the more heavily traveled paths. The no-name horse was well rested and eagerly maneuvered through the brush, as they came within sight of the big oak and the Dolin cabin.

Hunter pulled back the reins, coming to a stop as he combed the countryside for any movement. Satisfied there was no one about, he checked his guns, knowing full well they were at the ready, before continuing across the shallow part of the creek that ran off the main river.

He dismounted in front of the open barn doors and pulled his left-hand colt. Cocking the hammer back, the gunslinger entered cautiously to find the building empty. He gently released the revolver's hammer forward, sliding it back into its holster as he kneeled down, reading the story the tracks in the sand told him. There were extremely large, moccasin footprints that could only belong to one man. The man they had called Gator, who had been blown up with the Jackson hotel, which to Hunter seemed so very long ago.

He stood and followed the tracks to the edge of the hay, where he found dried blood that was now black. Farther up the hay pile, he spotted a ribbon. The same ribbon that had been woven through Lilith's hair the day she left town. The gunslinger bent down on one knee, picking up the red bow. He caressed it between his fingers and brought it up to his nose, inhaling its scent deeply. Tears did not come. He would not cry. The half-breed learned long ago men don't cry, they just make things right.

Hunter pocketed the memento and left the barn for the cabin. He walked across the lawn, glancing up at the gulls as he went. Without breaking his stride, he kicked in the front door, both pistols drawn and at the ready, only to find it empty.

How many times does a man have to kick in his own front door for fear of intruders? thought Hunter, before heading back outside where he began tracking Gator's trail, once again.

It led him back across the creek and to the north, in the direction of Frank Lugar's Ranch. As Hunter made his way up the path, he heard a distant rumble to the west. A wall of purple and black was approaching in the sky off the gulf. A huge storm was rolling in; this along with the coming of the night could give the gunslinger an advantage. The darkness would help keep him from being seen and the rain would help keep him from being heard.

◆❖◆

The storm came hard at first, blanketing the sun an hour before its usual time to set. The wind pushed the rain sideways, only seen through the darkness by the flashes of lightning which were followed quickly by the claps of thunder. It was slow moving for him, but he patiently continued on toward the ranch.

After a while the violence of the storm settled, leaving a steady downpour. Hunter could see the inner log fence that surrounded Lugar's ranch from where he had taken refuge, just inside the thick tree line of a patch of cypress. The half-breed removed his bow from the saddle, along with his remaining arrows. He wished he had taken the time to make more, but three would have to do. He left the horse behind, making his way on foot just inside the edge of the woods, weaving in and out through the numerous cypress trees. He took his time, resting against an occasional oak or pine.

The half-breed moved quickly, but silently, through the woods in short spurts as the Indians had for hundreds of years. With some help from a sustained flicker of lightning, he could see the main house. In a squatting position, he waited, surveying the area. Around the corner of the house, a guard appeared armed with a rifle, walking the railed porch that appeared to go all the way around the building.

Hunter nocked the arrow, pulling the string back to full draw. He aimed high on the man's neck, compensating for the distance and the heavy force of the rain. The shot would be a kill in the windpipe, inhibiting the man from yelling out and warning others.

He took a deep breath then released the arrow; it flew straight and true to hit its target dead center. The gunman's rifle dropped as he clutched his throat with both hands, before barrel-rolling head first over the rail to the wet ground below.

Death's a bitch, Hunter thought.

He immediately left the woods, launched himself over the waist-high fence. Then he sprinted twenty paces, jumping the porch rail at the back of the house. He nocked another arrow while making his way along the outer wall, stopping to peek around the corner.

Another guard stood smoking with his back to him.

Hunter loosed the arrow, hitting its target between the man's shoulder blades.

The shocked cowboy turned, raising his revolver toward Hunter.

With his last arrow, the half-breed shot the man's gun hand through the wrist, before the trigger could be pulled. The gun hit the wood porch flooring with a clank, followed by the dead man with a thud. Dropping the bow, the gunslinger pulled one of his .44s and worked his way across the grounds after leaving the porch. He ducked into the barn.

There was little moonlight and the hard rain gave effective cover for him to move around with little chance of being seen or heard. No one was watching the horses the barn held, eight well-broke cattle ponies in all. This gave Hunter an idea of the number of crackers he faced. With two men done for, that most likely meant there were six left.

With the boss gone, he figured they would most likely be holed up in the main house. Holstering the Colt, he pulled out the shotgun, breaking it open to make sure the shells were dry. Satisfied, he ventured out into the rainy night, leaving the cover of the barn heading toward the bunkhouse. Hunter glanced again at the two-story house, making a mental note that the upper windows were dark; the only light he could see was coming from the bottom floor.

The front door to the bunkhouse was closed but unlocked. Cautiously, he entered, making his way down the shadow-ridden hall. There were three doors on the right with one on the left. Hanging on the wall was a lantern which he lit with a wood match pulled from his coat pocket. He started for the first door on the right when he heard a sound coming from the door on his left. It sounded to him like labored breathing. Kicking in the door, Hunter swept the room with the scattergun at the ready, holding the lantern high with the other hand.

There, lying on a cot was Zeke, wheezing heavily, obviously burning up with fever. Hunter hung the light on a nail sticking out of the wall. Walking over to the boy's bedside, the gunslinger felt his forehead with the palm of his hand. He was hotter than a spent cartridge from Sam Colt's equalizer. The boy was unconscious and would die soon if he didn't get him some doctoring.

"Hang in there, little man," Hunter proclaimed quietly, "help's a' comin'."

With urgency, he left the room, setting the oil lamp on the floor in the middle of the hallway. He began kicking open the other three doors one at a time, with the double barrels pointing the way. The small rooms were all empty. The clock was ticking against the boy, so he hurried out into the rain, running straight for the main house. The gunslinger took the four steps two at a time, stopping only to peer through the front window. He saw one of the men sleeping in a chair by the fire. Quiet time was over.

Hunter shoved the shotgun through the window, breaking the glass pane, and fired one barrel, opening the man's chest before he knew what had happened. He sidestepped and fired the other barrel at the handles of the double front doors, blasting them open. Hunter holstered the shotgun without taking time to reload it and pulled both Colts, cocking the hammers back, as he entered the two-story home.

As soon as he stepped into the foyer, he heard boots running down the stairs; they then began firing directly in front of him. The shots rang out, and the gunslinger began firing as well. The sound was deafening, the room quickly filled with smoke as the flashes of the ignited gunpowder pushed the bullets out the barrels. A bullet scraped Hunter's right cheek, turning his head slightly. Another bullet nicked his elbow, almost making him drop his .44.

The fight was over as quickly as it had started. The half-breed's guns were empty, and when the smoke cleared, he could see two cowhands laying still on the stairway.

How many men left? Three, maybe four?

He stepped backward into the shadows in the corner of the room, putting his revolvers away. He loaded the shotgun as it was a faster reload than the Colts. This move turned out to be a good one. As soon as he slid in the second shell from his inside pocket, a man came through a doorway, firing wildly to his own demise. Hunter let him have both barrels from the side, taking the man off his feet and ending his life before he hit the floor.

The hot, smoky shells popped out as he broke the shotgun. With great speed, it was reloaded as were his Colts, all by feel. His eyes were panning around the room, looking for any sign of movement. The house was quiet.

He now took the time to assess his wounds. His right cheek had a slight burn to it and his elbow dripped blood, the bullet grazed the bone and hurt like hell, but all in all his injuries were minor. The five-day-old wounds on his side and leg had reopened from all his activity, turning his bandages red. He didn't believe the blood loss was significant. He still had his strength, after all, and his head remained clear. With his arms crossed, and a loaded colt in each hand, the gunslinger began sweeping the house for any others.

The storm was passing, giving the moonlight a chance to shine through the windows, making it easier to see. This allowed the gunslinger to move more quickly. He made it through the kitchen and into a back bedroom, when he heard the pounding hooves of horses on the run. He rushed to the window to see the remaining three men making their escape. Pulling out his pistols, he broke the glass and opened fire on the fleeing riders. He shot two in the back, making them tumble from their horses to the ground. The third got away, disappearing into the night. Hunter cursed. If he'd had his rifle with him, not one would have survived.

He searched the rest of the house including the upstairs to find out he was alone before he hurriedly made his way back to get his horse. He thought he knew which trail the old doc would be traveling on. It was a direct route north and the only path that would accommodate his rig. Doctor Harmon had a day's head start on them, but Hunter and Zeke could move faster than the wagon and would not be restricted to the roads and trails. Time was not on the boy's side, so he must move quickly.

After removing a section of fence to bring the Appaloosa through, Hunter tethered him to a post outside the bunkhouse and entered. The lantern still burned in the hallway. He snatched it up and went to the room where Zeke was laying.

The boy lay too still, his eyes wide open, and his brow no longer sweated. Like all the others that meant so much to Hunter, Zeke was dead. The gunslinger went to both knees and bowed his head having only one regret – there was no one left to kill. He took the lantern and slung it against the wall.

The flames erupted, immediately moving up and catching the ceiling, bringing it alive with the colors of red and orange. Hunter took one last look at Zeke before darting from the room and high-tailing it out of the building. He mounted the uneasy Appaloosa, who welcomed the boot heels to its sides as they took off at a dead run away from the wood structure now engulfed by fire. The smoke mushroomed to the sky, above a wall of flames.

Hiding behind a giant oak tree, Chin Yang watched as the gunslinger and his spotted horse disappeared into the cold wet darkness, not once looking back.

The half-breed gunslinger with the name Hunter James Dolin, beaten and battered, with new bloody wounds that would become old scars of the past, rode deep into the swamps on his trusty Appaloosa. He had finally been given a name. From now on, the horse would be called *Zeke*.

The gunslinger had one thing on his mind – hunt down, find, and kill the man who got away.

The End
(or is it?)

ABOUT THE AUTHOR

Bret Lee Hart, a second generation Floridian, has spent the last twenty-five years in Marine construction; he is married and the father of two. His mother's maiden name is Emerson, as in Ralph Waldo, and on his father's side, Edgar Allen Poe can be found hanging on the family tree. With this bloodline of writers, and being named after Bret Harte from his western short stories, it was inevitable his imagination would find its way into print.

The *Half-Breed Gunslinger*, *Hunter James Dolin (Book II)*, *Montgomery's Revenge (Book III)*, *Wanted Dead (Book IV)*, and *Wars End (Book V)* are the five books in this "cracker Western" series, as Bret calls them, and are available at major online book retailers.

The Fangslinger and the Preacher, Preacher Jack and the Fangslinger (Book II) are also available with many other adventures soon to be unleashed from this exciting storyteller's mind in various genres, including Fantasy and the Paranormal.

Follow Bret Lee Hart on Facebook:
https://facebook.com/bretleehart

OTHER WORKS AVAILABLE FROM BRET LEE HART

✳ ✳ ✳ ✳ ✳

~ A Western action adventure, the first in
"The Half-Breed Gunslinger" *series ~*

In 1860 there was more open range cattle in Florida than in Texas and all the other states combined. It took a special breed of man to live there, and an even harder man to survive. Hunter James Dolin, half white and half Indian, was such a man. He was a gambler by trade and a gunslinger of necessity and attracted trouble wherever he traveled. But with his two Colt Walkers and bowie knife, he could handle almost anything.

Brief excerpt:
About ninety miles back and a few days earlier, in the crackerjack Saloon along the Withlacoochee River, Dolin's ace-high straight flush had beat one of the three outlaws' full house. He won fair and square – two ounces of gold and a just 'broke in' Henry rifle. These days that was more than reason enough to kill a man.

Hunter had felt the itch in his craw that warned him he'd out-stayed his welcome, and knew it was high time for him to leave this place. Without taking his eyes off the men at the poker table, Hunter had gathered up his winnings, while he spoke, "Thank you, Gentlemen. It's been a pleasure."

The man at the table to Hunter's left, the one who just lost his Henry rifle, had stood and replied angrily, "Do you think we're just gonna let you walk on out of here, half-breed?"

＊ ＊ ＊ ＊ ＊

Spurred by revenge...
Gunfights and gold...
One man against the odds...

Hunter James Dolin survived the revenge war of Myakka City, Florida, by killing the men who raised their guns against him and his loved ones – all but one.

The Governor directed the Army to investigate, forcing the Half-Breed Gunslinger to seek refuge deep in the swamps of the Everglades.

Hunter James Dolin was content to live the rest of his life in solitude – 'til he was sought out and told of the whereabouts of the one that got away.

This would spark a new battle of revenge, overshadowed by the Civil War, but not soon forgotten by the people who inhabit the Florida swamplands.

Brief excerpt:

Scooter was swinging like a pendulum as very large Gators came up out of the water and snapped at the chicken, just out of reach of the man's head. Scooter was screaming again, as Hunter backed Zeke up a bit, putting his face and head closer to the teeth-laden jaws of the twelve-foot reptiles. The largest of the Gators stretched his neck up and snapped two pieces of chicken hanging down less than a foot from Scooter Johnson's head.

"PULL ME UP!!!! PULL ME UP!!!!" shrieked the dangling man. "I'm not the last – Montgomery's alive! *HE'S ALIVE, PLEASE!!!"*

Hunter urged the Appaloosa forward so the rope hanging over the branch moved with him, pulling Scooter up and out of reach of the Gator's bite.

"What do you mean, *he's alive?*" yelled Hunter. "I blowed him up in his own hotel."

✳ ✳ ✳ ✳ ✳

~ A Western action adventure, the third in "The Half-Breed Gunslinger" series, set in Florida. Author Bret Lee Hart reminds us his state was once as wild as the West – and just as deadly. ~

Duke Montgomery is an Indian fighter – a hard-as-nails killer, plain and simple – who doesn't think twice about ambushing a man or killing him face-to-face. When he learns his brother Richard is dead, killed by the Half-Breed Gunslinger, Duke goes on the hunt.

To avoid trouble after his dealings with Richard Montgomery, Hunter James Dolin and the woman, Helen, travel deep into the Everglades to live in peace for a while. But, as is the way of the world, trouble soon comes looking for them.

How many will die as Montgomery seeks the Half-Breed Gunslinger to get revenge? And what surprises are in store for Hunter James Dolin?

Brief Excerpt:
"Where you headed, mister?" asked Billy.

"Myakka City is my first stop," replied Duke.

"Where's that at, Billy?" whispered Junior, leaning toward Billy.

"Not sure," said Billy, "Where's that city at, Mister? Maybe we could tag along with yah?"

There it was; Duke had just recruited these two easily with his larger mind. He grabbed the whiskey bottle by its neck, and with the other hand chugged the last of his beer then slammed the glass mug on the counter. "We leave tomorrow mornin' at sunup, meet me at the hotel. You will be paid if you do your jobs and don't git yourself killed." Duke turned and headed for the door, taking his whiskey bottle with him.

"What might our jobs be?" said Billy to his back.

The shirtless, scarred, muscle man stopped and turned after two steps. "We're going to Florida to kill a stinkin' half-breed."

Billy and Junior looked at one another and grinned with confidence that the job would be easy enough.

"What do your friends call you, Mister?" Junior asked.

"I don't have any friends, but you will call me Sir." Duke turned and walked out, leaving the saloon doors swinging behind him.

* * * * *

~ A Western action adventure, the forth in
"The Half-Breed Gunslinger" *series, set in Florida.*

While *The Half-Breed Gunslinger* fights for his life against infection from a gunshot wound, there are wanted posters being printed with his name and likeness. A $5,000 bounty on the head of Hunter James Dolin is more than enough money to attract men to the swamps of south Florida. The ending of the Civil War turns soldiers into bounty hunters as the North feels the need to cleanse the South, and men find ways to make a living.

The gunslinger's woman carries his child; Helen will need help from their close friends as her pregnancy progresses. Jebidiah and Walt will protect Helen at all costs with their experience and grit. Bodie and Bird, with their own skills, will be by their side in whatever comes their way. To their surprise, unexpected rivals come after the newly named Dolin Family.

Brief excerpt:
"What's goin' on, Hunter? Talk to me."
"Bounty hunter keeping track of our whereabouts." Helen's hand went to the butt of her gun. "Easy, woman; he's gone for now, but he will be back and with friends."
"What will we do?" she asked calmly.
"We can't stay here, it's too open. We could hold them off inside the cabin but for only so long; eventually they would burn us out. Myakka City is where our friends are; they will increase our numbers."
"Then we'll git little James, Alameda and Mocha and go to town at once."
"It ain't safe for the boy or you. I think maybe you should take little James and go with Alameda to the Seminole tribe lands..." Before he could finish, Helen was on her feet and shaking her head.
"I will not stay with that Sam Jones; Alameda can take little James and Mocha out there but I will go where you go." She turned and began walking up the bank to the cabin. "We best git packin'."
Hunter knew Helen meant to stand firm on her decision and there was nothing he could say to change her mind once she had made it. The boy would be safest with the tribe and Helen's skill with the gun would be handy. She had been battle tested and had killed without prejudice. She would be more dangerous now that she was a mother, like a mamma bear protecting her cub.

✳ ✳ ✳ ✳ ✳

*~ A Western action adventure, the fifth in
"The Half-Breed Gunslinger" series, set in Florida.*

The three year Montgomery/ Dolin War was over, and not one family member named Montgomery was left alive. Hunter James Dolin had killed Richard Montgomery, his brother Duke Montgomery and their sister Jane Montgomery. The next man in line named Little Owl, for Chief of the Snake Clan of the Miccosukee, of the Seminole Indian Tribe was killed by the hand of the Half-Breed Gunslinger. Little Owl and his loyal braves were no more.

Myakka City and the James family had survived the last battle and Helen and little James were found alive at the waters' edge. Their current enemies were dead but Hunter was concerned about the wanted posters. There was no way to know how many had been printed and how far they had spread? The authors of the prints were dead but it would take time for this to be known and then believed. Five thousand dollars was a world of money and there would be men coming to kill the Half-breed Gunslinger and seeking their fortune.

Brief excerpt:
"The knife," said Hooker.

Hunter reached back and pulled the bowie from the sheath that was clipped to his pants at his back. Daryl took that too, with the same grin, only bigger.

"You take good care of that, Daryl; I will be needin' that back."

The stare of the gunslinger's steel blue eyes froze Daryl for a moment. His smile faded and then came back, but only a little.

"Oh, you won't need this no more, half-breed, not where you goin'."

"Daryl! I'm only gonna tell yah one more time to shut the hell up," the Captain warned. "Jimbo, tie his hands in the front; he's got to ride."

The big mouth drover picked up Hunter's pistol belt from the floor as Jimbo escorted the gunslinger outside. Zeke was there, and Hunter was placed on his back by two of the men.

"Where we headed, Captain?" Hunter asked.

"Daryl and Jimbo here will take you to Fort Foster and we'll let the army decide your fate."

"What of my family, Captain?" Hunter asked.

"When they are ready for travel I will personally escort them wherever they would like to go, unharmed. I give you my word as a lawman and a gentleman."

"You do as you say, Captain, and I will allow you to live. I give you my word, but your men here, a pass will not be givin'."

Jimbo glared at Hunter and Daryl laughed out loud.

"Let's go, tough guy," Jimbo replied.

"You try anythin', half-breed, and I'll kill yah with your own guns," Daryl said while resting his hand on Hunter's 44s that he now wore on his hip.

Hunter was glad to see his bowie knife tucked in the man's belt for he would need it as well on his return.

* * * * *

*~ A Paranormal Western based on the
age-old battle of good versus evil ~*

Master Andelko Balas is the leader of a bored, and therefore troublesome, vampire coven in Romania in the 1880s. Colonel Richard Andersson brings relief to the boredom by discovering tales of the American West and setting the coven on an exciting, but bloody, journey to a new land.

Jack Denton, reformed gunfighter, former preacher, now a drunkard, has visions of a great evil coming to Arizona as he wanders in the desert. Then he meets an Indian Chief and is given a silver sword, a special cross, and a mission. Jack is led to Black Mountain Mesa where an unusual storm is brewing and he has to face the greatest battle of his life.

Is this the last battle for the world as he knows it? Will his renewed faith and special weapons be enough to defeat such evil?

Brief Excerpt:
Black Mesa Mountain, Arizona, 1885
He went by the name Preacher Jack, given to him by his small congregation in New Mexico. He had buried the name Anderson in the past, going by the name Jack Denton in fear of being discovered by the law, or the lawless. It was a simple life he now led, and a good life for Preacher Jack, until God's plan for him continued forward. When his wife and daughter died from disease that swept through the small Mexican village, Jack lost his faith in God and left New Mexico, wandering aimlessly, not caring if he lived or died. Forty-year-old Jack Denton, a fallen preacher, was now a faithless drunkard living off whiskey – his only thoughts were of drinking himself to death.

Forty days and forty nights into his journey of despair, Jack found refuge in an abandoned mining shack to get some rest. A vision appeared to him as he slept, the drunken haze in which he slumbered left him, allowing the vivid images of his dream to come forth...

Fear overwhelmed him as something that Jack could only describe as a demon straight from hell swooped down on top of him, baring bloody fangs to devour his flesh.

Jack Denton awoke with a scream from the dirt floor of the mining shack.

✳ ✳ ✳ ✳ ✳

~ The Paranormal Western sequel to
"The Fangslinger and the Preacher" ~

Preacher Jack and his comrade Richard, a centuries-old Romanian soldier, thought their battle against evil was won after their climactic battle with the master vampire Andelko Balas at the top of Black Mountain Mesa. But Richard's former master was not vanquished permanently; the Fallen One has raised him up, and now Balas has an undead army at his command. The Preacher and the Fangslinger, aided by the mystical Indian White Owl and his followers, are now all that stands in the way of the vampire master's plan to empower his dark lord and unleash hell on earth.

Will the Preacher's faith be strong enough to sustain them?

Brief Excerpt:

On his return to camp, Jack was surprised to see that Richard had pulled himself up and was now leaning against a flat rock formation alongside the campsite that partially blocked the dry desert wind. As Jack got closer he could see that the color in Richard's face was much better. Jack then realized that the colonel had positioned himself in a shady spot to avoid the rays of the morning light. This concerned the Preacher, for this was something a man with the blood of a vampire might do.

"Does the sun bother you?" Jack asked.

"Slightly, yes," answered Richard, "may I bother you for some additional water?"

Jack fetched the canteen and went to one knee as he handed it over, but this time Jack did so at a greater distance.

Richard took several small sips, and then the two men stared at one another for a moment.

"You do not trust me so?"

"Ain't sure just yet," answered Jack, "you did save my life on that mountain, and the rumor is that we are kin, but the simple fact that you're hidin' from the sun does got me wonderin'."